She sat up straight.
"What are you doing here?"

"It's our wedding night—remember?"
Brandon sat down on the edge of the bed and
brushed a wisp of hair back from her cheek.

"But you said you weren't interested in going
to bed with me," Carey said, her voice small
and breathless. "You said...."

"You assumed that I wasn't interested. You
piqued my interest the day you turned me
down. You made me determined to have
you." He let a finger slide gently down her
throat. "Besides, an empire isn't worth
building unless a man has a son to leave it to."

Her mind frantically played back everything
he'd said on that fateful day. The treach⸺ ̣ ̣s
sneak! He just hadn't ̣ ̣ ̣ ̣
intended to s ̣ ̣ ̣ ̣
have been so ̣ ̣ ̣

Books by Leigh Michaels

HARLEQUIN ROMANCES
2657—ON SEPTEMBER HILL

HARLEQUIN PRESENTS
702—KISS YESTERDAY GOODBYE

These books may be available at your local bookseller.

For a list of all titles currently available,
send your name and address to:

Harlequin Reader Service
P.O. Box 52040, Phoenix, AZ 85072-2040
Canadian address: P.O. Box 2800, Postal Station A,
5170 Yonge St., Willowdale, Ont. M2N 5T5

On September Hill

Leigh Michaels

Harlequin Books

TORONTO • NEW YORK • LONDON
AMSTERDAM • PARIS • SYDNEY • HAMBURG
STOCKHOLM • ATHENS • TOKYO • MILAN

Original hardcover edition published in 1984
by Mills & Boon Limited

ISBN 0-373-02657-9

Harlequin Romance first edition November 1984

For my family at Harold Hughes Hall
Who helped me learn
that serenity lies within my reach

———————————————◆———————————————

CHAPTER ONE

CAREY Forsythe's high-heeled sandals tapped briskly down the long corridor, but the sound died abruptly as she stepped on to the deep plush carpet inside the office suite.

The walnut door hadn't swung shut behind her yet when the secretary at the big desk looked up from her typewriter and said, 'Mr Dennis is on the phone. Would you like him to hold for you?'

Carey nodded. 'Yes, please. Just give me a minute first.' She was patting her chestnut hair, neat in a smooth French twist, as she spoke, making sure there wasn't a strand out of place.

'I'll buzz you as soon as he's finished talking to Mr Mason. Your coffee is on your desk.'

Carey paused on the threshold of her employer's office and sniffed the air. Even a full week after Clarke Dennis had collapsed and been hospitalised, she could still smell his aftershave here in his private sanctum. It bothered her that Clarke's secretary referred to it so easily as 'your office', 'your desk'. After all, it wasn't as though Clarke Dennis wouldn't be coming back to the executive suite. She pushed away the wave of doubt that threatened to choke her—Clarke was, she had to remember, nearly sixty—and sat down in the big leather chair.

A chime sounded discreetly on the desk, and Carey reached for the phone. 'How are you feeling this morning, Clarke?'

'Oh, I'm considerably improved. It helped my state of mind when they moved me out of intensive care and told me it isn't my heart this time. I don't mind telling you they had me worried.'

'And all of us, too. What is it, then?'

'They're still not sure. I'll have more tests later today. And they told me it will be a while before I can come back to work, regardless of what it is. But since you and Doug are there, I have nothing to worry about.'

'Well—Doug is doing fine; let's leave it at that. I'll plan to stop by this afternoon, now that you're allowed visitors.'

'Good. It gets lonely in here. As a matter of fact, I really wanted to ask you for a favour.'

'Of course, Clarke. What is it?'

'Do you have a date this evening?'

'No, not a date. But Lynne's coming back from a long flight this evening, and we had planned to go to Donalan's to see the new bridal fashions.'

'I can understand why you want to see your sister. Who's shopping for a wedding gown?'

'Lynne, of course. I'm nowhere near that stage, and I probably never will be.'

'It won't be for lack of opportunity—and that's the only compliment you're going to dig out of me today, Carey. Actually the fashion show would be ideal for what I have in mind. Let me ask you anyway, and then you can say no if you like. I really want you to get my wife out of this hospital for a while. She's been here night and day for a week, and if she doesn't relax soon they're going to have to find us a double room.'

And it isn't doing you any good, either, is it? Carey said to herself. Worrying about his wife was only adding to Clarke's load.

Clarke went on. 'Nancie loves Donalan's fashion shows; she never misses one if she's in town. Tell me, Carey, could you do that? Or would Lynne mind too much?'

Bless Clarke; he always gave her a graceful way out. It was a quality she had never found before in an employer, and it was one of the main reasons she was still Clarke's administrative assistant. 'No, I'm sure Lynne wouldn't mind. She was in for three days last week, so we got a lot of talking done then. At least, Lynne did. I'd be happy to have Mrs Dennis with us, if she'll agree to it.'

'Good girl. I'll work on it.'

'I'll see you late this afternoon, then.' Carey put the phone down and sat for a moment puzzling over her action. She adored Clarke Dennis, but she had little use for his wife. So why had she let herself in for a whole evening? Well, if it helped Clarke relax, it was well worth it. And at least Lynne wouldn't be able to spend the whole evening complaining again—it was the only thing she'd been doing for weeks.

Actually, Carey told herself, she had no reason to resent Clarke's wife. She had only met Nancie Dennis a couple of times. In the year that she had worked for Clarke, Carey had just happened to be out of the office on the rare occasions Nancie came in. To be perfectly honest, she supposed, she had to admit that she was jealous of Nancie—of the fact that Clarke had married at all.

In their childhood she and Lynne had grown to love him as though he had actually been their uncle as well as a good friend to their perpetually irresponsible father. Clarke had always been there when they needed him, and nothing was ever more important to him than they were. Then their father had moved them to another state, and they had lost contact with Clarke. But it had seemed only natural for Carey to return to St. Louis, where she had been born, and train to be a stewardess in the airline Clarke owned. And just as natural for Lynne to follow in her sister's steps.

Clarke had spent a year trying to convince Carey that she was wasting time pinning souvenir wings on spoiled brats and serving whisky sours to flirtacious businessmen, that her intelligence and experience cried out to be in administration. Finally she had agreed and had taken the job as Clarke's administrative assistant.

It was about that time she had first realised Clarke had got married, and she had felt betrayed. For no good reason, of course; even Lynnne had told her that. She couldn't even say that Clarke had chosen unwisely, for

Nancie Dennis was a lady from the top of her expen-sively-coiffured hair to the toes of her handmade shoes. But Carey still couldn't accept the woman, and so she studiously avoided her. It seemed as though Nancie wasn't anxious to get to know Carey, either, for though Clarke occasionally took her out to dinner, Nancie was never there, and Carey had never been invited to their home.

Carey reached for her coffee cup, sipped, and made a face. She had let it get cold. She started to go through the mail, which was mostly routine; at least, thank heaven, Doug Mason, who was Clarke's second-in-command, had the headaches of daily operation.

She reached for the intercom and asked the secretary to bring her a fresh cup of coffee. Instead, it was Doug who brought it.

'What are you doing here?' Carey asked. 'I thought acting vice-presidents had their coffee brought to them, not the other way around.'

Doug threw himself down in the chair beside her desk. 'I come bearing gifts because I need to ask a favour.'

Carey looked him over warily. 'Everybody needs a favour today,' she said dryly. 'What is it, Douglas?'

'I don't want to have lunch upstairs today, dear. Would you go?'

Carey considered reminding him that she hated to be called 'dear', but decided it wasn't worth the bother. She and Doug had been through the whole equal-rights argu-ment so often it was becoming a bore. So she tackled the more important question. 'I don't want to have lunch upstairs today, Doug. You know how I feel about the big boss.'

'Of course I know—you tell me frequently,' Doug said, rolling his eyes towards the ceiling as he remem-bered the details. 'But I am going to meet an informant who can tell me why the baggage handlers are ready to strike, whereas you are free to go charm Mr Scott.'

Carey absently reached into her desk drawer and pulled out a nail file. She drew it viciously across a manicured nail.

Doug grinned. 'Sharpening your claws, Carey? Besides, I went last week; it's your turn. Equal rights bring equal responsibilities, you know.'

Carey examined the damage she had just done to the nail and sighed. 'All right, I'll go. But you owe me,' she said acidly.

'Anything you like,' he agreed cheerfully. 'Go charm the socks off him.'

'His socks are not what I'm worried about.'

Doug grinned and then turned it into a leer. He probably knew just as much about Brandon Scott's reputation as any man in the whole Scott Enterprises empire. And, like most of them, Carey thought, he probably had a secret wish that he dared live the way the boss did. 'Are you still holding out, Carey?' Doug chided. 'As Brandon himself has no doubt told you—why be prejudiced against a man just because he has more money than is good for him?'

'Oh, I'm not prejudiced against him because of the money. There isn't one thing about the man I like. He's a chauvinist, a dirty old man, a . . .'

Doug cut her tirade off with the ease of long practice. 'Carey, we've been through all this before. In the first place, he isn't more than thirty-five, and that is not old. In the second place, not even you can hold a grudge for ever. The man made that pass before he found out that under your provocative surface lies an unliberated body.'

'Provocative? I wear tailored suits!'

'Honey, face the truth. You'd be provocative in long red flannel underwear. Add that to the fact that you're always agitating for equal treatment for women, and it's no wonder old B.S. got the wrong idea.'

'So it's my fault that he made a pass at me?'

'Of course not. But it isn't exactly his fault either that a skirt can't go by without him chasing it.'

'I find it very hard to believe that he has no choice in the matter.'

'Well—maybe you're right. In any case, his prowling days are almost over. Rumour has it that he's about to take a dive into matrimony.'

'I can't imagine it'll end his prowling,' Carey said tartly.

'Oh, she's worth what he's giving up.'

Carey didn't answer, but her silence was disapproving.

Doug laughed. 'You don't want to hear any more? All right. I shouldn't gossip anyway, so I won't go on.' He pulled himself out of the comfortable chair.

'Of course I want to know! Who is she?'

'Michelle Lantry. Surely you recognise the name?'

'She's the fashion model trying to become a Hollywood star, isn't she?'

'That's the one. I wonder if she'll give up her career. I always imagined Mrs Scott would be expected to stay home and mother little Scotts. And of course they won't have any trouble living on what he makes.'

'I can't imagine him as a father,' Carey snapped. 'I pity his poor kids. Or see her as a mother, either—being pregnant would ruin her figure.'

'Have you ever seen her?'

'Only on magazine covers.'

'I have. She's got some figure—it would be a shame to ruin it.' Doug paused at the door to wave a casual hand. 'Have a nice lunch, Carey!'

The food was delicious, but that was about the only advantage of going to the weekly luncheon where the vice-presidents of the company gathered to make their reports to Brandon Scott. He was a scrupulously fair but demanding employer, and if one of the companies under the umbrella of Scott Enterprises wasn't doing as well as he expected, the head of the business had better be prepared to explain the lack. Sometimes, it seemed to Carey, the vice-presidents were carved up even more than the roast beef. It was far from being a casual three-martini get-together to chat about business trends.

Universal Airlines was only a recent addition to the Scott empire. Barely six weeks after Carey had left her air hostess days behind and come into the main office, Clarke had sold controlling interest of the airline to Brandon Scott, and they had moved into the central administration building. The new office quarters were plush; the bronze glass and steel building with its floors of shops, apartments, and offices wasn't the largest in St. Louis, and it was no competition whatever for skyscrapers in bigger cities, but it was one of the most beautiful—designed by one of the world's premier architects to be a proud addition to the city's skyline.

The salary scale for Universal's staff was also improved when the airline came under the corporate umbrella, but the first time Carey had met Brandon Scott she had decided the old days had been infinitely preferable. In fact, long-time loyalty to Clarke was all that had kept her from finding another job.

As the uniformed maid removed her table setting and replaced it with coffee, Carey let her mind wander from the discussion going on in the formal dining room back to the day of her first vice-presidents' luncheon with Brandon Scott.

Clarke and Doug had both been out of town, so as the one left in charge, Carey had put in an appearance. It had been just a few weeks after the move, and she was still a bit uncertain in her new job.

After the discussion was over, the rest of the group had quickly scattered, relieved to have the luncheon behind them for another week, but Brandon had stopped Carey before she could leave the dining room. 'Clarke's been keeping you so busy down there, we haven't had a chance to get acquainted,' he said. 'Would you stay a few minutes?'

She agreed, flattered to be singled out since she was only a third-level employee. She was also a bit nervous. Had he purposely waited until Clarke wasn't there to defend her?

Brandon took her out on the wide terrace that overlooked St. Louis. The sun was warm and brilliant on the glass and steel. Just a few blocks away sunlight glinted off the mirror-smooth stainless steel of the six-hundred-foot-high Gateway Arch, its slender frame looking impossibly frail from this distance. It stood as it had for years, a memorial to the Louisiana Purchase of 1803 and the daring westward expansion of a brash new nation. Beyond the Arch lay the sparkling water of the Mississippi River, wending its implacable way towards New Orleans and the Gulf of Mexico.

St. Louis was a city that was still spreading out rather than climbing up, and from the terrace on top of the office building the city sprawled over the rolling Missouri hills like an animated patchwork quilt.

The breeze teased at Carey's hair. 'It's lovely,' she said. 'I've been up higher, of course, in the Arch, but never on such a clear day.'

'And the windows are always dirty,' he said.

'I wouldn't want the job of cleaning them on the outside, though,' Carey laughed.

'No, and I wouldn't like to be the one who climbs out on top to replace the bulbs in the aircraft warning lights, either,' he agreed. He looked out over the city, his eyes half closed against the brilliant light. 'My view is beautiful, isn't it?' he mused, and turned back to her. 'And so are you.'

She turned her head, shocked and surprised, thinking that she must have heard him wrong. Whatever she had expected, it had not been that. And while she had become adept at turning aside passes in her air hostess days, she had not expected to need that skill here.

'Surely someone has told you that before?' he asked, gently brushing a tendril of hair back from her cheek. 'They must have, Carey, because it's true.'

She was silent, still stunned and wondering what the right response would be, and he interpreted her silence as willingness. Before she could make another move, he was kissing her, his mouth gentle, then growing insistent. Her lips parted under his, and he deepened the kiss, his lips exploring the sweetness of her. He pulled her closer, moulding her slender body against the hardness of his.

Carey had known her share of kisses, but never before one that made her feel as if lightning was flickering along every nerve. Her head was spinning, and she wanted the kiss to go on for ever.

Then from some distant compartment of her mind, reason returned. What was she doing, standing here and letting her employer kiss her with the intimacy of a lover? She was not the kind of woman who was willing to earn her position with her body. She placed both hands on his chest and pushed. Her action took him off guard and he let her go.

Carey put out both hands to steady herself against the terrace rail and, still half stunned by the assault on her senses, said the first thing that came into her mind. 'Does this have anything to do with whether I keep my job?' she snapped.

'Of course not.' He sounded a little surprised.

'Good. Then let's not do it again.' And she turned to stalk back across the terrace towards the French doors which opened off the dining room.

Brandon caught her, seizing her elbow and planting his other hand against the door so that she couldn't open it. 'Don't get so upset, Carey. If I'd known you were frozen solid, I'd have built a bigger fire,' he said smoothly.

Carey was silent, thankful that he didn't realise how close she had been to losing control.

'You might like to tidy your hair a little before we go in. You look a bit ruffled, and I'm sure you wouldn't want the rumour-mill to see that. How long is your hair, anyway? Do you always wear it up?'

'That's none of your business,' Carey said curtly.

He smiled and watched her smooth her hair, then said, 'When you change your mind, honey, I'll be here.'

'Don't bet on me changing my mind.'

His velvet brown eyes summed her up. 'You'll thaw,

Carey.'

'About the same time Siberia becomes a tropical resort,' she said flatly.

She had felt those brown eyes boring into her until she left the office suite and sank weakly into a corner of the elevator on the way back to her own office. And still, whenever she met Brandon Scott, he would look at her wickedly, and his eyes would say, 'You'll thaw.'

The pity was that she wasn't able to ignore him. He was too darned attractive for that, with thick dark hair and those deep brown eyes that had a way of glinting in amusement whenever he looked at Carey. When he looked at her, she couldn't help remembering the hardness of his body against hers and the pressure of his mouth, and the wild madness of those few moments before sanity had returned.

She supposed he did find her refusal amusing. After all, most women would have seized the opportunity to be his mistress. Brandon Scott was one of the Midwest's wealthiest men. And, unlike most rich men, he was both young and attractive. He had been a millionaire before he was thirty, and now he seemed to be determined to own St. Louis. After he had as much of Missouri as he wanted to own, Carey supposed, he'd start to really expand his empire.

He worked hard, and he played hard. The women he was pictured with were always draped in jewels and designer clothes. They must be an expensive hobby, Carey thought, and was outraged afresh at the idea that he classified her with them, that he expected her to fall into line. There were things more important to her than a man's bank account, qualities that Brandon Scott probably didn't even know about. No matter how rich he was, it would never give him the right to look at her in that coolly assessing way every time they met.

As he was looking at her right now, she realised with a start as her mind came back to the meeting. The man sitting next to her was talking about production quotas, but Brandon Scott's eyes were resting on Carey. She pretended not to notice his gaze, picked up her cup, and scalded her mouth. Out of the corner of her eye she saw him start to smile.

'That's a good report, John,' he said. 'You're doing some splendid work down there. Carey, how is Clarke doing?'

'As of this morning, he seems much improved. But there is still nothing definite about what is wrong with him or when he'll be able to come back to work.'

He seemed uninterested; Carey realised he had already known exactly how Clarke was feeling. Of course he would, she told herself; Clarke was an important cog in this business. She doubted that Brandon Scott would have disturbed himself over the matter had Clarke not been a vice-president.

'And how is Universal doing?' he asked.

'Very well. Doug is working through an informant on a possible strike by the baggage handlers. He isn't sure how serious a threat it is, but he wanted to investigate it before it had a chance to develop. That's why he isn't here today.'

Brandon smiled. 'I knew there had to be a good reason.' Under the smooth voice, only Carey heard what he was really saying. He knew quite well that she avoided him whenever possible, and it was just another of the things about her that amused him.

She ignored the comment and went on, 'We're working on some new promotions to pull passengers away from other airlines this winter—some packages and special rates. I'm negotiating with a hotel chain nationwide to allow us to combine air fare and room charges, and that should make a tempting package. We have several good possibilities, and we'll be ready to present some firm plans next week. Everything is under control.'

'I'm sure it is in good hands. Bob, how is . . .'

Carey tuned out again and heaved an inward sigh of relief. Why did she always feel like a third grader on the carpet in the principal's office whenever he said anything to her? He was only a man, even if he was a powerful one.

Yes, but if he decided that teasing her about that stolen kiss wasn't fun any more, he could tell Clarke to fire her. And certainly she could sue because she was discriminated against, but what good would that do her?

'Did you want to speak to me privately?' Brandon asked.

Carey jumped. She had been lost in her thoughts, staring into her coffee cup, while the others were leaving the table. 'No.'

'We could go into my living room, if you'd like.' There was a smile in his voice.

'No, thanks. I'd like to still have a reputation when I leave here,' she said tartly, and set her cup down with a firm little click.

Brandon laughed. 'Are you ever going to forgive me my trespasses, Carey? After all, it was only a kiss.'

'Good day, Mr Scott,' she said, and brushed past him.

CHAPTER TWO

SHE hadn't seen Clarke since the day he had called her into his office to say he didn't feel well, and then passed out as she stood there. He looked better, his white hair combed neatly and his shocking pink silk pyjamas reflecting some colour into his face.

Carey giggled and tugged at the pink sleeve. 'Don't try to tell me the hospital issued you these!' she teased and leaned down to kiss his cheek.

Clarke laid his magazine aside and took his glasses off. 'You look contented, my dear. Universal doesn't seem to be getting you down.'

'How could it? Doug's doing all of the work. I'm just intercepting your phone calls and thinking up new ways to draw passengers. The regular routine.'

'Well, don't let it run you, you run it. Nancie's gone down to get a cup of coffee. She said she was beginning to feel the strain. I think she'll go to the fashion show, but I'll leave it to you to offer the invitation, if you want to.'

Carey started to protest. 'Of course I will . . .'

Clarke looked her over. 'I'm not blind, Carey. I don't understand why, but I know you've been avoiding Nancie. And I'm certainly not going to force you into each other's company. I want you to be friends.'

Carey opened her mouth to answer, but Clarke didn't give her a chance. 'How is Lynne? She never stops in to see me, you know. And who is the young man she's marrying?'

'Lynne's fine; you know she always manages to take care of herself. She's marrying David Stratton. The on-again, off-again romance is back on.'

'He's the pilot, isn't he?'

'That's the one. I hope they make it this time. But

19

Lynne's working a job you couldn't pay me enough to take.'

'What is it? She's still with Universal, isn't she?'

'Oh, yes. She loves the so-called glamour of being an air hostess. It amazes me, though, that she gets along so well with the passengers when she's such a spoiled brat the rest of the time.' Carey sat down next to Clarke's bed. 'She's on Mr Scott's private jet. It's a temporary assignment, but Lynne's hoping to make it permanent.'

'That explains why you wouldn't take it. I wish I knew what Brandon did to get on your wrong side, Carey, but it can't have been that bad.'

'Oh, really?' Carey asked dryly.

'Really. Here comes Nancie.'

Carey looked up to see a tall, platinum-haired woman come in. Her first impression, as on their first meeting, was of enormous blue eyes; then the design of the sapphire-blue trouser suit Nancie Dennis wore, and the obviously hand-tooled leather bag she carried, registered. Carey was no fool, and she knew what clothes like that cost. No wonder Clarke was in the hospital, she thought. He must be working terribly hard to keep Nancie dressed in style.

Nancie tossed her bag on to a chair and bent over to brush Clarke's cheek with her lips.

'How was your coffee, dear?' he asked.

'A poor substitute for Scotch—but it woke me up. Hello, Carey.'

Carey rose and put out a hand. 'It's nice to see you again, Mrs Dennis.'

'But a shame that it had to be in a hospital room. Next time I'll insist that Clarke brings you home for dinner. You've known him for a long time, haven't you?'

'For ever, more or less,' Carey said.

'I resent that,' Clarke protested.

'Well, I was only eight or nine . . .'

'And I suppose you're a senior citizen now,' he said derisively, and laughed.

A nurse came into the room and asked them to wait

outside for a few minutes while she took a blood sample. They walked slowly down the hall, and Nancie started to talk as if the words were being forced from her. 'You're so good for him, Carey. He hasn't laughed in the whole week he's been here, until you came in.'

'I don't imagine there was much to laugh about when he was in intensive care. He's been very ill, hasn't he?'

Nancie nodded and stopped to lean against a wall, her eyes closed. Without the flashing smile, Carey could see strain written deep around her mouth. 'At first they thought it was a massive heart attack. At least that's what I was afraid of. Now they're not sure what it was, but at least it wasn't his heart.' She opened her eyes and smiled wanly.

Carey's heart went out to her. So she did love Clarke after all. She heard herself say, 'Mrs Dennis, I think you need to get away from the hospital for a while. I'm going downtown in a little while to meet my sister. We're going to Donalan's fashion show; he's showing all the new bridal gowns today. Would you like to come with us?'

'Oh, that sounds . . . But Clarke . . .'

'Clarke's fine. He can manage without you this evening. If you don't relax you're going to end up in bed yourself, and then what good could you do? I'll bet you haven't been home more than a couple of hours a day since he collapsed.'

Nancie smiled wryly. 'You're right about that. And I would like to see the bridal show; it's my favourite of all of them. If Clarke doesn't mind being left alone, and if you're sure I wouldn't be intruding, I'll come.'

'There is no intrusion. Lynne would love having expert advice. Not that she's expecting to buy her dress at Donalan's, but she's looking for ideas.'

Clarke winked at Carey over his wife's shoulder as he gave his approval. 'And then I want you to go straight home and to bed, Nan,' he said. 'You need your sleep, and I feel as though I could drop off right now.'

As they were getting into Carey's car in the parking lot, Nancie asked, 'You did say it is your sister who is shopping for a wedding gown?'

'Yes. She's an air hostess, and she's engaged to one of Universal's pilots.'

'They'll have a lot in common.'

'I just hope they make it to the altar this time. They've been living together off and on for a year, and it's wearing me out.'

Nancie sighed. 'Perhaps I'm old-fashioned, but I still prefer it when the couple buys the marriage licence before the bedroom set. And you—are you shopping?'

'Just browsing.'

'Anybody special in mind?'

'Oh . . . Maybe.'

'If he's only a maybe, he isn't the one.'

Carey laughed but wouldn't comment. 'There's my sister, Mrs Dennis. She's hard to miss in that Universal uniform.'

'Yes. They're distinctive, that gold and green combination, but, do you know, I've never liked them. Why don't you try to talk Clarke into letting you redesign them? And by the way, if you can call him Clarke, you can surely call me Nancie, can't you?'

'I'd like that, Nancie.' There was a warmth about the woman today, a humanness, that had been missing before, and Carey found it reassuring.

As they came up to the unostentatious entrance to Donalan's shop, Lynne turned to meet them with a swirl of her forest-green cape. 'There you are, Carey. It's chilly out here, and I've been waiting an age!' Her voice carried a sharp note, something almost hysterical.

What was bothering Lynne now, Carey wondered. But once inside the shop, Lynne seemed to relax.

The maitre d' didn't even ask to see their invitations, and he nearly fell over himself to get them to a good table. Carey fleetingly wondered why. Then she remembered her own reaction to the cut of Nancie's clothes—obviously the woman was well known here.

Lynne looked around at the well-dressed women surrounding them. 'I feel so out of place in uniform,' she complained. 'But there just wasn't time to change. Or at least I didn't think there was time. I didn't expect you to be late.' Her glance at Carey was furious. Carey felt like reminding her of the numerous times that Lynne had breezed in half an hour behind schedule without a word of apology.

'You look lovely,' Nancie said. 'And don't feel out of place. I came straight from the hospital and Carey from the office, so you aren't alone.'

'But your outfit probably came from here in the first place, and Carey doesn't exactly buy her clothes at Woolworths, either.'

The room darkened, and the spotlights played over the long catwalk. They had a perfectly situated table with the best view in the house, and Carey made a mental note to invite Nancie any time she wanted to really see a fashion show again.

The first few gowns were modelled to the accompaniment of Lynne cataloguing their flaws. 'This is obviously the wrong year for me to get married,' she decided. 'Everything is ruffled, and all those frills would made me look like a plastic doll.'

Carey wondered when there would be a good year for Lynne to be married, and then decided to ignore her sister. She sipped her tea and nibbled at a tiny sandwich, and practised the art of ignoring Lynne. If she listened to her, her own enjoyment would be spoiled, and she wanted to enjoy the show.

As always, wedding gowns had a predictable effect on her—she'd been bridal-gown crazy since she was tiny. Carey could vaguely remember being held up by her mother to admire the first bride Carey had ever seen. She must have been three years old, and it was still one of her strongest memories. And even now, though she knew it was silly, all she had to do was see a wedding gown and she could picture herself in it, walking up the aisle to meet—whom?

That was the tricky question right now. Carey was not really in a hurry to be married, but she was twenty-five now and starting to think that if she was to have her own home and the family she wanted, she shouldn't wait too long to start. Lately she had been dating Doug Mason, but it didn't seem to be developing into anything, and she wasn't sure she wanted it to. And now and then Lynne would come up with a pilot friend of David's who needed a date, but most of them were too much like David for Carey's taste. Besides, when they found out what her job was it scared most of them away. It was sad, but still true, that having a better job than a man you were dating was not a good step towards a lasting relationship. Especially when it was in the same organisation.

'That's more like it,' Lynne declared.

Carey studied the gown and agreed, thinking that clothing was one of the few things they thought alike on. The dress was very simple, with a wisp of a veil instead of the elaborate headpieces the other dresses had featured. And it was probably three times the price Lynne could afford.

'Oh, well, at least a girl can dream,' Lynne said finally. But her voice did not sound resigned.

Nancie lifted a hand and a fresh pot of tea arrived. 'Have you looked into designer patterns?' she asked. 'Perhaps you can have your designer gown by having someone sew it for you.'

'It would be marvellous to walk down the aisle in a Donalan gown,' Lynne mused. 'Even if it had to be a fake one. Thanks, Nancie, I'll look into that.'

Then the lights dimmed again and shifted, and the music changed. 'Here it comes,' Nancie said. 'For every collection, Donalan designs one dress that is absolutely not for sale. It's always the last to be shown, and it's always incredible. He usually gives it to a museum, or something, but people come to these shows just to see the dress that no one can buy.'

'I've heard that, but I've never seen one before,' Carey said.

The curtains were drawn back and a pencil-slim model came out on to the catwalk. Her gown was cream-coloured, not white, of the shiniest satin Carey had ever seen. The bodice was tightly fitted, and the skirt fell in wide, heavy pleats to a chapel train. The sleeves were long and fitted to flaring cuffs. It was a dress that would be cruel to an imperfect figure, showing every flaw. But on the model, it was superb.

The girl passed so close to Carey that she could hear the whisper of the satin and see the detail of the fine lace that trimmed the neckline, the cuffs, the hem, relieving the severity of the satin.

'That's a dress for a princess,' Lynne whispered.

The veil was nothing but a drift of illusion, edged in lace. The headpiece was a satin bow that nestled at the crown of the model's head, allowing the veil to drift down as if weightless, but leaving most of her glorious red hair displayed.

Carey found her hand pressed to her throat as if to still the pulse that was pounding there. She glanced over to find Nancie's eyes on her.

'It takes people that way sometimes,' Nancie said with a smile.

Carey laughed shakily. 'It was so beautiful, it made me want to cry.' She cast another wistful look at the model, who was retreating backstage.

'Not for sale, hmm? Why not? He could get thousands for that dress,' Lynne mused.

'He's been heard to say that once in a while he just has to design something without worrying what it will look like on an overweight, frumpy matron. Or in this case, an overweight, pimply teenager, I presume.' Nancie sipped her tea.

Lynne laughed. 'It's a law of life that only overweight matrons can afford that sort of thing, isn't it?'

'Wouldn't Carey look pretty in it?'

'Unfortunately, it would take a couple of years' salary, even if it was for sale,' Carey said regretfully. 'And remember, Nancie, I'm not even shopping!'

The wind was blowing stronger when they came out of

Donalan's shop, and Lynne gasped as it caught at her cape. 'I hope you're taking me home, Carey,' she said. 'I don't want to ride a bus in this.'

Carey nodded. 'Of course, Lynne. I go right by your apartment anyway. Would you like to have dinner, Nancie?'

Nancie glanced at her watch. 'No, thank you. I'll just have a sandwich at home and call Clarke. And he was right, I feel as if an early night would be a good idea. Thank you for making me come, Carey. It has relaxed me.'

She declined a ride and hailed a cab instead. As soon as she was gone, Lynne got into Carey's car, pulled her beret off and sank wearily back against the seat. 'I wish I could afford to live like that,' she muttered. 'I wish I could see the bill for her clothes in a year.'

'I don't think I'd like to know,' Carey said.

Lynne ignored the comment. 'Why did you have to drag Nancie along tonight, of all nights?' she complained. 'Carey, I'm in trouble, and you may be the only one who can help me out of it.'

This, then, was what she had felt when she first saw Lynne outside the shop. Something was bothering her and, as always, she had brought it to her older sister to have it solved. If it had waited this long, Carey thought, it would wait a few minutes longer. 'Would you like to stop for something to eat?'

'I'm too tired to bother—I want to go home and take a hot bath and collapse. I wouldn't have come at all if I hadn't had to talk to you.'

Carey pulled out of the parking lot and turned towards Lynne's apartment. 'What's the trouble?'

'It just happened this afternoon. The whole week since I started flying on Brandon Scott's jet we've been ferrying the social leaders around. What a bore! And he hasn't been near the plane himself the whole time.'

'That would be a comfort unless you wanted to flirt with him.' She glanced at her sister. 'But you would, wouldn't you, Lynne? I warn you, you'd be playing with fire.'

'Oh, he's nothing I couldn't handle. All men are alike, Carey. All it takes is a little charming willingness and you can get anything you want from them. But you're too much of a prude to ever do anything like that, aren't you?'

'I suppose that's one way to think of it,' Carey agreed calmly. 'Wouldn't David mind if you had an affair with Brandon Scott?'

'Oh, he understands the advantages; he's on the plane too.' Lynne shrugged it off. 'Just look what I could get from it.'

'We'd quarrel if I told you,' Carey said dryly. 'I don't think you know Mr Scott very well if you think he's going to be enchanted by charming willingness, as you put it.'

'Mr Scott,' Lynne mimicked. 'You certainly haven't taken advantage of your opportunities, have you, Carey? I'd have thought that working in the same building, you'd have seen some advantage in getting to know him better. Give me six months on that plane, and I'll have him eating out of my hand.'

'You might succeed in interesting him, but I doubt it would last more than a few days.' And then, no doubt, Lynne would come crying to her to have the situation fixed. 'Lynne, let's not spend any more time on a fruitless discussion. Go on—you've been transporting the social leaders, you said.'

'Mrs Harrison Ayres was on board today. Do you know her?'

'Not personally, no, only from the newspapers. She's quite the thing in local society, isn't she?'

'I suppose so. Though why, I'll never understand. She has no taste; today she was wearing a perfectly awful necklace—a gigantic emerald set in amethysts.'

'Purple and green?'

'Cross my heart. She went to sleep in her seat—she snores, too—and when she woke up, the necklace was gone.'

'Lost?'

'Stolen, she said. I told her it must have had a loose catch and fallen off. But Her High and Mightiness said none of her jewellery ever had loose catches. And it went on and on till we were about to land.'

'Has it been found?'

'Oh, yes.'

'Then I'm sorry, but I don't see the problem.'

Lynne sat up. 'It was in my flight bag,' she said wearily.

'In your . . . but how?'

'I don't know. I've asked myself a thousand times. I can't think of a reason that anybody would steal such a thing, especially from right around her neck like that. Taking a piece of jewellery out of someone's luggage—that's different; it might not be missed.' She shook her head. 'But to risk taking the chain from around her neck! And especially Millicent Ayres. If anybody would notice, it would be her.'

'How did it get into your bag?'

'It's a safe bet that it didn't walk there by itself. And it's also a safe bet that Mrs Ayres didn't accidentally mistake my flight bag for her Gucci original.'

'So somebody put it there.'

'They must have, Carey.'

'What do you want me to do?' Carey asked, after a moment.

'Mrs Ayres is apparently a very close friend of Brandon Scott, and she has threatened to tell him the whole ridiculous story and demand that I be fired and prosecuted for theft. She was standing there screaming and waving her arms . . . I tell you, Carey, if David hadn't been on that flight I'd be in a hospital right now, and you know what kind I mean.'

'Yes, I can picture that,' Carey said dryly. She could see Lynne going off into hysterics, especially if there was a man present to bring her out of it. It was too bad for Lynne's plans that Brandon Scott hadn't been a passenger on his jet today—she would no doubt have fainted right into his arms. Carey parked the car in front of Lynne's apartment building. 'Well, I'll do what I can.'

'Thanks, Carey.' It was perfunctory—Lynne had had no doubt that her sister would come to her rescue.

'Do you want me to come up, or will you be all right alone?'

'David's there—I'll be fine.' She wrinkled her nose. 'He's going fishing this weekend, though. That's when I'll be lonely. I'll probably go crazy up there by myself, and we're not scheduled to fly again until Tuesday.'

'Sounds like an exciting way to spend a weekend.'

'Fishing? It drives me nuts. But one of his buddies has a river cabin, and they've been going up whenever they can. I guess as long as he doesn't insist that I come along, I can put up with it.'

'How is David?' Carey's question was polite and not particularly interested. David Stratton was just the sort of man she had always expected Lynne to marry: portrait-handsome and, she suspected, just as self-centred under the charming surface as Lynne herself was.

'He's fine. He's so happy I'm with him on the executive jet, and it really is marvellous duty, Carey. You will be able to fix it all so that I can be on it permanently, won't you?'

'I'll see what I can do. My powers are not unlimited, you know.' Carey hesitated. 'Lynne? You didn't take the necklace, did you?'

'Carey!' Lynne's voice was ragged with hysteria. 'How can you say such a thing? Don't you believe me?'

'I had to ask, Lynne.'

Lynne looked at her coldly and said sharply. 'No, I didn't take it.' Then she got out of the car and slammed the door.

CHAPTER THREE

CAREY dressed especially carefully the next morning, one because she might have to make an appearance in Brandon Scott's office, and two because the longer she took to get to work, the longer such an appearance could be postponed.

Her tweed suit was expertly tailored, complete with a waistcoat to add to the appearance of the totally professional woman, and it was perfect for a fall day which promised to be crisp before evening. The mauve blouse picked up one of the muted shades of the tweed. It reflected some colour into her face, and the ruffle at the neckline softened the severity of the jacket. The suit was part of her new autumn wardrobe, and it had cost the earth.

She was a little uncertain of what Lynne expected her to do, she thought as she applied a touch of blusher to her cheekbones. She could bring the matter to Brandon's attention, but what if he hadn't heard about it already? What if Mrs Ayres' threat hadn't been carried out? Wouldn't telling him just be asking for Lynne to be fired?

But if she waited, the damage would be done before she had any chance to counter it. She applied mascara and thought it over. Losing her job would devastate Lynne.

Carey arrived at the office with her mind still not made up. She was tense and nervous and kept having to do things over again. The promotional packages that she was supposed to be getting ready for the vice-presidents' luncheon next week still lay untouched on top of her desk at noon.

It was almost a relief when Brandon's private secretary called and said that he wanted to see her in his office right after lunch.

Her own secretary brought her soup and a sandwich, but Carey couldn't force the food down. Finally, she pushed the plate aside and started for the penthouse floor.

She was left to wait in the reception room for a while. She toyed with a magazine for a few minutes, scarcely seeing the print. What she really wanted to do was get up and pace the floor, but with two secretaries in the room it was hardly the self-possessed thing to do.

One of the girls was a casual friend; they sat together in the employees' lunchroom sometimes. She gave Carey a sympathetic smile, but it only made Carey feel worse. How much did the secretary know, she wondered. Was she sympathetic because Carey was going to have to face the boss alone, or did the girl know something big was about to happen?

What was taking so long, she wondered. But of course, she told herself, what happens to Lynne is only a minor irritation at Scott Enterprises, hardly worth the head man's time. Of course, a moment of Brandon Scott's time could ruin Lynne's life—but then Carey didn't expect that fact to weigh heavily with him. She supposed she should feel grateful that he had been thoughtful enough to consult her—he could have just fired Lynne outright.

The door to the inner office swung open and a man in a plaid suit appeared. He said, over his shoulder, 'Well, you think about it, Scott, and when you decide to buy that property, let me know. But don't wait too long because the price may go up!' He let the door close and came across the reception room, bestowing a wolfish smile on the secretary who handed him his hat. Then he stopped beside Carey, grinned, and said, 'Well! I didn't expect to find you here.'

Carey looked past him. 'I think you're mistaken. We haven't met.'

'Shall we take care of the details now?'

The secretary said. 'Miss Forsythe, you may go in

now.'

Carey walked across the room, scarcely hearing the wolf as he said, 'Can't win them all.' But she was so righteously indignant about him that she scarcely remembered why she was in the office at all.

Even through her anger, though, she had to be impressed with the private office she was ushered into. She had never been in it before, as the other meetings she had attended had been either in the dining room or one of the conference rooms. This office was painted, rather than panelled, in a warm shade of ivory that made a good background for some beautiful art objects. The man had good taste, she had to admit. Then came the thought, I'll bet he didn't choose these things himself!

Brandon Scott was seated at the mahogany desk, with a folder open on the blotter before him. He looked up as she approached the desk, removed dark-framed reading glasses, and stood up to greet her.

He was wearing a dark brown suit which emphasised the breadth of his shoulders and which tapered to a lean waist and hips. His blindingly white shirt contrasted sharply with the tan that had lasted through the fall. He really was devastatingly good-looking, Carey thought absently. Then she caught herself up short. She was here to defend Lynne, and allowing herself to be sidetracked wouldn't help anyone.

He came around the desk and indicated a comfortable couch, then sat down opposite her on the corner of a table. Instantly, Carey felt that she had been put on the defensive.

'I have some unpleasant news for you today,' he said. When Carey didn't answer, he went on, 'It concerns a Lynne Forsythe—who surely must be your sister?'

'Yes.'

'I had a visit this morning from a friend, Millicent Ayres. It seems she lost a piece of valuable jewellery yesterday while she was on my private plane, and it was found in your sister's luggage.'

Carey was silent.

He lifted an eyebrow and said, 'You don't appear to be surprised. Does she make a habit of this sort of thing?'

'Of course not! Lynne told me about it last night, and I was just considering whether it's worth my time to repeat it to you. It seems as though you have convicted her unheard.'

'Since I'm paying for your time right now, let's hear the story.' His voice was inflexible.

'Lynne doesn't know how the necklace got into her flight bag. She did not take it, and she doesn't understand why anyone would steal it, since the theft was certain to be discovered. No one would be dumb enough to take such a thing and hide it in her own bag.'

He started to laugh. 'Or perhaps someone would be smart enough to do just that. Next you'll be telling me that it didn't disappear at all!'

'Is it so hard to believe that someone else would pick it up and drop it into Lynne's bag? They might have done it to throw suspicion on her, or in the hope that she would carry it off the plane before the theft was discovered.'

'Yes, it's hard to believe. One thing you don't know, Carey, and that perhaps your sister didn't know either, is that all of that crew, with the sole exception of your sister, have been on that plane for at least a year without an incident.'

'And my sister has been with this airline for several years without an incident!' Carey flared. 'Doesn't that count for something?'

'Not for much,' Brandon said dryly. 'She would hardly have this sort of temptation thrown in her path on ordinary flights.'

'Is there anything I could say that would make you believe me? Why did you call me up here, anyway, if you weren't prepared to listen to anything I might say?'

He ignored the question. 'I think it is necessary to turn the matter over to the authorities for a decision on whether Lynne should be prosecuted. It goes without saying that she will never fly for Universal again.'

'She couldn't be convicted on the flimsy scraps of evidence you have!'

'People have been hanged on less,' he pointed out.

'Isn't she entitled to the benefit of the doubt?'

'Perhaps. But that will be for the authorities to decide. If they choose not to prosecute, she'll have a reference, but not a job with Universal.'

'Why don't you just limit her to regular flights? You said yourself that the temptation wouldn't be there.'

'Oh, so you're afraid she did take the necklace?'

'I am not! But it would be better than being dragged through the courts and falsely prosecuted. Even if she's acquitted it will follow her for ever.'

'You sound very doubtful that the outcome would be positive for Lynne.' He idly swung a foot, and Carey couldn't help noticing that the shoe was custom-made.

'I don't give much for her chances if you're on the other side,' she said bitterly.

'Do I hear a note of grudging respect? That's a change, from you, Carey.'

'Grudging, certainly. Respect? I have no respect for you.'

He was silent for a few moments, as though studying her suggestions. Then, when she had just begun to allow herself to hope, he shook his head. 'No. I'm afraid I just couldn't do that. It wouldn't be fair to future passengers not to have it investigated.' He was silent again. 'Unless . . . Unless we could make a kind of a deal.'

Carey felt herself shrinking back into the couch cushions. 'What kind of a deal?'

He smiled, and those velvety eyes roamed over her. 'Surely you have some imagination, Carey?'

Carey felt as though she were a butterfly struggling to escape, waiting hopelessly for the pinch that would end its life.

'You want me to go to bed with you, I suppose, in

return for your forgetting about the difficulty Lynne's got herself into.' Carey stood up and paced across to the wide windows. 'What choice have you left me? She's my sister, and it's her career at stake. All right; I'll do it. So why don't we get it over with right now, so that I don't have to think about it any more?' She unbuttoned her jacket and slipped it off, tossing it on to a nearby chair. 'Which way do I go to reach your infamous bedroom? It must come in handy—and probably makes doing business a real pleasure!'

'Just a minute, spitfire,' he said, and amazingly, he was laughing. 'If you think you're calling my bluff, you're wrong. That wasn't quite what I had in mind.'

Carey felt like a fool. 'It wasn't?'

'No,' he said gently. 'So why don't you put your jacket back on . . . No, on second thoughts, I like you much better without it—you look much more feminine and a lot more approachable. Let me hang the jacket up. Now sit down, and we'll have coffee and talk.'

He must have ordered the coffee earlier, for it was only moments before the uniformed maid carried in an elaborate silver tray and coffee service. Carey was startled to see something so ornate in an office.

Brandon said, 'We'll pour for ourselves, thank you,' and waited until the maid was out of the room before adding, with a sidelong glance at Carey, 'We could have gone into the apartment, but I'm sure you'll be more comfortable remaining here. As for the coffee service, haven't you noticed by now that I'm not the complete barbarian you thought I was? Will you pour?'

She did, admiring the way the heavy old silver pot balanced in her hand. 'I admit that you have good taste in coffee services—if you chose it yourself, of course. Cream and sugar?'

'Just sugar—two lumps. I picked up the silver service in Vienna a couple of years ago. All by myself.' He stirred his coffee.

Carey poured her own into the eggshell china and silver filigree cup and added cream. She hadn't met his eyes since her threat to undress. Even thinking about that brought a flush to her cheeks. She knew his eyes were on her, and she felt as though he were looking right through her.

'Are you interested in a little deal?'

'I suppose for my sister's sake I have to be, don't I?'

'I think you'll find it has certain advantages for you, too, Carey,' he said dryly. 'Let me tell you what I have in mind. I have a house out on the west side, near Forest Park . . .'

Carey shifted uneasily in her chair.

He grinned. 'Don't get all tensed up yet, Carey. It's a big house, and it takes a lot of looking after. Right now, it seems to be going downhill. I have a housekeeper and a butler and half a dozen maids, but it isn't good enough—they don't have a personal feeling for the house. For years my mother was my hostess and looked after the place. But since she remarried it's just too much for her to handle. I need someone to take her place. What I'm really proposing to you is a job change.'

'I don't quite see where this fits in with Lynne and me.' Carey sipped her coffee and tried to sound uninterested.

'Remember that I have been looking for a long time. I have high standards. The woman I'm looking for must have intelligence. People talk about dumb blondes being housewives, and perhaps they are, but not good ones. To run a house like mine requires an executive; someone every bit as professional as you are. That's what I need: a woman who can entertain at parties and be at ease in social situations, who can make my guests comfortable, and who can keep my home running smoothly and make it a peaceful place I want to come to at the end of a long day. A professional homemaker, if you will. I've been watching you since I bought Universal. With your training, poise, and intelligence, you'd be perfect.'

'Why tie it in with Lynne?'

He held out his cup and she refilled it. 'I am under no illusions as to what you think of me, Carey. If I had called you up here and offered you this job, you'd have said no so loudly the entire building would have heard. I'm not above making a bargain when it's to my advantage. At least you heard me out this way.'

She thoughtfully refilled her own cup. This didn't sound like a trade-off, it sounded like a dream job. And while she was certain that if she turned him down he would not show mercy to Lynne, it still sounded as if she would be giving up very little. It had taken the last week without Clarke Dennis running Universal to convince her that she did not want to do that all of her life. But running a house, especially a big house—that was something Carey had always planned to do some day. To get paid for it was the icing on the cake.

But it just didn't ring true.

'Aren't you afraid I'll swipe the ladies' jewels at your parties?' she asked sarcastically.

He smiled. 'Of course not. I already know that you have good taste in clothes—that suit didn't come off the bargain rack. You'll have everything you could possible want—clothes, jewellery, all of the accessories—as my wife.'

Wife? 'Oh, no! No, no, no.' Carey stood up and put the table between them.

'Oh, come and sit down. Carey, admit that you were intrigued by the idea until that nasty four-letter word *wife* came up. So what is the problem?'

'Why do you want a wife? I can't imagine you, with the reputation you have, worrying about the conventions. There are plenty of girls out there who would faint even if you gave them so much as a cross-eyed look. Why do you have to pick on me? What Lynne might or might not have done isn't that bad.'

He winced. 'Do you have to be so flattering? It's mostly because I'm tired of all the girls. You're right, there are plenty of them, if you'll pardon the immodesty. I'm tired of the gossip columns speculating if I'm getting serious every time I take one of them out the second time. Besides, most women bore me. I don't think there has been one born who could hold my attention for ever.'

'My question stands—why me?'

'I'll be blunt. If I marry any one of the women I've been dating, she's going to be jealous of my work and of the occasional woman I will find interesting. She will expect me to devote every free moment to her and to let my business slide. I haven't time to spend winters in Bermuda and summers in Monte Carlo.'

'Maybe she'd rather go alone, anyway,' Carey interjected sweetly.

He ignored her. 'On the other hand, if I marry you, you will understand from the beginning that this is a business deal and my work comes first. You won't interfere with either my work or my recreation. You'll just be doing your job. I'll end up with the best of both worlds.'

'Why get married at all? You sound awfully cold-blooded about the whole idea.'

'I told you, Carey. Every time I take a woman out I see her calculating how to trap me into marrying her.'

'My heart bleeds for you.' Solicitude was noticebly lacking in Carey's voice. 'Do you really think they won't be doing that if you're wearing a wedding ring? Or do you expect me to walk around with a shotgun, defending you?'

He smiled. 'Most of them would consider you to be daunting competition, with or without the shotgun.'

Carey was startled by the underlying seriousness of his voice. She wasn't at all bad-looking, she knew, but the idea that she could compete with some of the lovely women she had seen pictured with him was laughable. 'Sorry. I'm honoured, of course.' Her voice dripped sarcasm. 'But I think I can live without the pleasure.'

Brandon shrugged and set his cup back on the tray. 'It's your choice, of course, Carey. I certainly can't force you. I'll have my secretary call the authorities and give them the details. I'm sure Millicent Ayres will be anxious to talk to them.'

'That is blackmail!'

'An ugly word, don't you think?' He went over to his

desk and took some snapshots from a drawer. 'This is my house—it's called September Hill.'

Carey took the photos unwillingly. 'That's an interesting name.'

'My mother named it. She first saw the site at the end of September, in a year when fall came very early. It was all ablaze with red and gold leaves as it is again now.'

Carey leafed through the pictures without comment, then put them on the table. 'Let's not be patronising any more about letting me choose what I'm going to do. You aren't giving me any choice, and you know it. So let's get things clear. Do you promise that if I marry you, there will be no charges filed against Lynne?'

'None.'

'Can you swear to that?'

'There will be a letter in the mail to Millicent tonight telling her that I've taken care of the situation.'

'Will Lynne have a job?'

'As long as she's a good little girl from now on. She'll be on regular flights, of course—no more playing about on my plane.'

'Fair enough. And nothing will go on her personnel record?'

'Not the slightest smear.'

'And all I have to do is be a glorified housekeeper, give your parties, and look the other way when you find a rare, interesting woman.' Her voice was sarcastic, but underneath it shook a little.

He nodded. 'That's it.'

'Well, looking the other way will come easy enough. How long is this little masquerade going to last?'

'Oh, let's put it on the same basis as box seats at the opera—renewable annually.'

'What you really mean is that you have the option, and I don't.'

His smile flashed. 'You're quick, Carey. Of course the option is mine. But just think of the position you'll have. You'll be a leader of society, and you'll have all of the trappings of wealth—jewellery, clothes, a chauffeur.

With that kind of a deal, why would you want to back out?'

'You said there hadn't been a woman born who could hold your attention for ever. I'd hardly want to try, but how long do you think I'll last?'

'Oh, much longer than if this was an ordinary love affair. As you said, you'll just be a glorified house-keeper, really. And business deals have a lot more stamina than romance does.'

'It says a lot for the state of romance in this society,' Carey murmured.

'Besides, you won't be giving me the jealous act if I look at another woman—jealousy is the first thing that turns me off. So I'd say three years, maybe. Who knows? You might be lucky. You'd get severance pay of a sort, by the way.'

Carey considered that for a few minutes. 'And the alternative? If I don't marry you?'

'Poor Lynne. I'm sure there's an airline somewhere that would hire her without a reference.'

Carey was silent. What choice did she have? It had always been up to her to get Lynne out of her scrapes. It just seemed that this time the price was a little higher than usual. She said sarcastically, 'Under the circum-stances, Mr Scott, I am delighted to accept your very flattering proposal.'

'Under the circumstances, Miss Forsythe, I am honoured.' He reached into his pocket. 'I hope this is the right size.' He snapped open a velvet box.

Carey couldn't help gasping. There, in the tiny case, lay an enormous marquise diamond set in platinum and surrounded by tiny sapphires.

'You're sure of yourself, aren't you?' she snapped.

'Self-confidence pays, my dear,' he said. 'The setting matches your eyes—I do hope you like it.' He picked up her hand to slip the ring on.

'What if I don't like it?' She pulled away.

He recaptured her hand and put the ring firmly on her finger. 'You'll learn to, I'm sure.'

'Do I have to wear this? It's a farce. Surely you don't need to add this to it.'

He frowned. 'Let's get one thing straight right now, Carey. You're going to be my wife, and I will give you anything I please. I will not permit my wife to be out-done by anyone.'

Carey nodded meekly. So she was just another art object, was she? Just like the silver service.

'It will be unnecessary for you to come back to work. I'll let Clarke know. Other than that, unless you have objections, I'd like to keep it fairly quiet. Shall we schedule our wedding for a week from today?'

What difference did it make which day she went to the electric chair? And it wouldn't do any good to argue; he'd made up his mind. Carey agreed mechanically.

'Tomorrow I'd like you to have lunch with my mother at September Hill. She'll show you over the house, and she will probably have some suggestions for your shop-ping. My car will pick you up at your apartment.'

Carey let the words flow around her, not really know-ing what he was saying. She felt as if she had been caught up in a flood of raging water that was sweeping her along, unable to keep her head above the surface. But finally he stood up, dismissing her, and she was free to leave the penthouse floor.

CHAPTER FOUR

CAREY had had nightmares in which she was running from some unseen danger, something too unspeakable to face. But not even that gave her the same feeling of being pursued that she had now as the elevator whirred down to the main floor. She half expected Brandon Scott to materialise inside the elevator with more demands.

She stepped out into the three-storey atrium lobby, with its splashing fountains and lush green plants, scarcely aware of where she was. The only thing she really noticed was the weight of the ring on her left hand. It felt like a bowling ball dragging her arm down.

Suddenly hands grasped her firmly by the shoulders, and Doug Mason said, 'What's the matter, love? Are you all right?'

'Yes. No,' Carey said, and sagged against him.

'Have you been to the infirmary?'

'No.'

'Then let's go.'

'No! Just take me home, please.' Then a vision floated through her mind of herself telling the company doctors why she was so upset, and Carey started to laugh.

'Carey! Settle down. You're going to pieces in the main lobby. Don't have hysterics on me, honey, please.'

'Such a pity Mr Scott's not here to see,' she muttered. Hadn't he said something about poise being a great qualification for her new position?

'What did you say? Something about the boss? No wonder you're so upset. Did he make another pass or something?'

'Or something,' Carey admitted.

But Doug was more interested in reaching Carey's car without drawing any more attention, and he didn't notice that she hadn't really answered his question.

'Where's the key, sweetheart?'

She fumbled through her handbag. 'Here. I'm all right, Doug, really. I can get myself home.'

'Yeah. Sure.' He put her in the passenger seat and got behind the wheel. 'You're just fine, and the Queen of Switzerland wears a beard.'

'Silly—there's no Queen of Switzerland.'

'That sounds better. I was beginning to think there was no Carey Forsythe, either—just a bunch of pieces like a jigsaw puzzle.' The car pulled out of the parking lot and joined the stream of traffic on the boulevard.

'I'll be all right.' As soon as I've had a year or two to adjust, she thought.

'That's my girl. Don't let it get you down. Whatever it is.' He reached down to pat her hand. 'New ring? You haven't been wearing one on your left hand.'

How was she supposed to answer that, Carey wondered, and parried for time. 'I'm surprised you noticed.'

'I always notice. Some guys watch ankles, some watch knees, some watch . . . Well, anyway, I watch left hands.'

'Isn't that a little discriminatory?'

'I haven't had any objections from right hands yet. You're sounding better.' He took his eyes off the traffic for a moment to look at her.

'I'm feeling a little better.'

'I'll take you to lunch at Angelo's tomorrow if you come back to work. That should be an incentive—I really am going to need you.'

Carey felt a stab of guilt. Doug was already carrying Clarke's load as well as his own. To have her leave unexpectedly would really pile the responsibility on him. But, she told herself, it wasn't her idea, and it wasn't her fault. There wasn't anything she could have done to change Brandon Scott's mind.

'I don't think I'll be in tomorrow.'

Doug ignored the traffic to look her over. 'Are you seriously ill?'

'No.' Tell him, Carey, she ordered herself. You've

been dating him for six months, and even if there has been nothing firm about your relationship, you owe it to him to break the news yourself, not wait until the formal announcement is made. But how?

She could say, 'Sorry, Doug, I can't see you any more, I'm marrying my local blackmailer.' Or, 'See you around, Doug; Brandon Scott finally made me an offer I couldn't refuse.' Or, 'You see, Doug, my new ring is really an elegant handcuff.'

No. Perhaps it was chicken of her not to tell Doug that this time next week she would be Mrs Brandon Scott, but she couldn't do it to him. She couldn't announce it to anyone, at least not until she had stopped thinking of it as a nightmare.

Finally she said, 'I'm just taking a day off for personal reasons, Doug. How are you going to get back to work?'

'I'll flag a cab as soon as I'm sure you're all right.'

'I'm fine now.'

'Don't snap my head off.'

'Then can we talk about something else?'

'You talked to Clarke today, didn't you? Did he tell you when he'll be back to work?'

'Another couple of weeks at least; that was the impression I got. All they know yet is what isn't wrong with him, not what is.'

'It can't be too soon for me.' He swung the car into Carey's spot, in front of the big apartment house. 'Do you want me to come up?'

'No, I'll be fine, and you'd better get back to work.'

'I'll tell your secretary you'll be back the day after tomorrow.'

'She's not my secretary—she's Clarke's. And don't be too definite.'

Doug looked at her speculatively. 'Are you quitting?'

'Not exactly.'

'You spent an awful lot of time in the penthouse this afternoon. Are you and B.S. drinking tea together these days?'

'No. Coffee, as a matter of fact.' Carey's voice was

tart.

'Can you give us an up-to-date description of his private little apartment? I've never talked to anyone who's actually been there.'

'You still haven't, Doug.' Why had she even thought of confiding in him?

'You didn't get fired, did you, Carey?'

'Of course not. Look, I'll talk to you later, all right?'

Doug wasn't satisfied with her answer, but just then Carey spotted a rare cruising taxi. 'Here,' he said as she turned towards the building. 'Here's a magazine you might like—something to keep you company this afternoon. I bought it because Michelle Lantry is on the cover.'

Oh, yes, she thought, the model Brandon Scott is going to marry. For an instant it actually didn't sink in. 'I'll get it back to you, Doug.'

'Don't bother; I've read all I was interested in. The lovely Michelle is just as gorgeous as ever. But you look as if you could use some cheering up. According to that story, your trouble with old B.S. will soon be over.'

It wasn't until then that it hit her. Her troubles with Brandon Scott would probably never be over.

'I wouldn't expect a little thing like marriage to change him, Doug,' she said, but his cab had already pulled into the traffic.

Carey lay awake till the night was far gone, then slept heavily and woke unrefreshed to the sound of the doorbell. When she stumbled to the door, she found a florist's delivery boy there. She signed for the long box and took it into the kitchenette. He was really doing it up brown to send flowers, she thought, and remembered what he had said about no one outdoing his wife.

But the roses weren't from Brandon. She sniffed the deep red blooms, their velvety petals bearing waterdrops, and pulled out the card.

'My dear Carey,' it said. 'We are delighted that you

and Brandon are to be married. Please allow us the pleasure of providing your gown as our gift to the daughter we never had. Love, Clarke and Nancie.'

'News certainly spreads quickly, doesn't it?' Carey muttered. Brandon had obviously been as good as his word about letting Clarke know that she wouldn't be in the office any more. She wondered if he had also told Doug, and wished again that she had had the courage to do it herself.

She arranged the flowers in a crystal vase and rushed to get ready for lunch. She discarded four outfits before settling on a simple green wool dress with a matching coat. It emphasised the auburn highlights in her hair and flattered the creamy smoothness of her skin.

'If your wardrobe doesn't lean to designer fashions when you're out to impress someone,' she told her reflection in the mirror, 'you have to stick to something simple.'

Then a thought hit her. What if she went all out to impress Brandon's mother—the wrong way? She pictured to herself what the woman must be like: starched-stiff and proper, and no doubt already upset at the idea that her future daughter-in-law was a career woman who had not been a débutante. If she played on that resentment . . . It should not be hard to convince the woman that Carey would not be a good addition to the family. His mother had seemed to be very important to him, Carey thought. If his mother objected, he would certainly break off this whole ridiculous mess. Wouldn't he?

But if she set out to do that, he would certainly discover what had happened. And since it would be Carey's doing, he would really be angry, and Lynne would be back in danger.

The car was waiting outside her apartment building—a dark green Lincoln town car, long and luxurious. The chauffeur, in matching green uniform, touched his cap as he helped Carey in.

It wasn't far to September Hill, as distance went, but in terms of standard of living, the trip carried her from blocks of pressed-together apartment complexes to estates set far back on wide lawns along a quiet avenue. Her first view of September Hill was breathtaking. Between towering old oaks peeked a large Georgian-style house built of yellow-gold brick. It was two-and-a-half storeys high, with enormous windows. The car passed through a wrought-iron gate in a brick wall that matched the house and slid noiselessly through a garden that was a riot of autumnal colours, to the front door.

The great door was opened just as the chauffeur helped her out of the car. Carey nervously clutched her handbag and started up the steps. Why was it so important that this woman liked her? For Lynne's sake, Carey reminded herself. For Lynne.

'If you'll come this way, Miss Forsythe,' the butler said politely. 'Mrs Dennis is waiting for you in the small morning room.' He relieved her of the wool coat.

'Mrs Dennis?' What did that mean? But before she got an answer, Carey was at the door of a bright, sunny room, and Nancie Dennis was rising to greet her.

'Welcome to September Hill, Carey!' she said, coming forward to offer an affectionate hug. Then, as Carey remained unresponsive, Nancie stepped back, and her eyes narrowed. 'Why, you poor child! Didn't Clarke ever tell you? Or Brandon? Didn't you know that Brandon is my son? Oh, wait until I get hold of those two! They let you come out here alone, expecting to meet some kind of ogre who wanted to look you over on approval . . .'

Carey protested faintly.

Nancie sighed. 'They'll hear about it,' she promised. 'Come and sit down now, and we'll have a good chat before lunch. Brandon tells me we have just six days before the big event. I must say it doesn't surprise me. He always makes up his mind quickly and expects everyone else to jump to attention.' She urged Carey along with an arm about her. 'We thought perhaps a very small group of guests for the ceremony itself, but then a fairly large reception immediately following. Right here at the house, unless you'd rather be married somewhere else?'

Carey agreed, wondering what had happened to Brandon's plans for a quiet wedding. Then she answered her own question—his mother now had a hand in it.

'Will Clarke be out of hospital in time to give me away?' she asked, with a vague hope that if he wouldn't be, Brandon might be persuaded to delay the wedding. Then she realised that nothing would change his plans.

'Yes, he will, and he'll be delighted that you've asked him, I'm sure.'

'Do the doctors know what's wrong with him?'

'They've concluded that he has a disorder in the amount of blood sugar, and he'll have to be on a strict diet to control it. That was all. Such a little thing, it seems, to have caused all of this fuss. But it's something we can live with.'

'I'm so glad it wasn't serious.'

'It will be good to have him home again, although he won't be back to work for a month or more while they get his diet regulated. But he needs the vacation anyway. Carey, can you have your list ready by tomorrow of the people you'd like to invite to the ceremony and the reception?'

'That should be no problem—there won't be many.'

'On such short notice, it may be a small crowd, but I imagine there will still be plenty of people who won't believe Brandon's married unless they see for themselves.'

'I think I know a few of them,' Carey commented.

Nancie just smiled. 'I'm planning to have Brandon's secretaries just start telephoning everyone. There isn't any point in trying to get invitations engraved and mailed. Then we'll send announcements, of course, to satisfy etiquette. Carey, I hope you don't mind if I take over like this?'

'Mind? I'm delighted. I wouldn't have any idea where to start.'

'When Brandon called me yesterday you could have knocked me over with a feather. I had no idea what was going on. And I don't imagine, knowing my son, that he gave you much more time to get used to the idea.'

Carey smiled. 'You're right.'

'And what about your gown? We'd like to surprise you with it.'

'I'd appreciate it very much.'

'I really meant it, you know. I'd like you to be the daughter I've always wanted. Clarke's always thought of you as his own, I know, and now with Brandon . . . I'd like it to be that way, Carey.'

It was touching that Nancie was willing to take her on faith, and to consider her as a daughter. How different this woman was from the starched matron Carey had expected to find! At least I'll be lucky in my mother-in-law, Carey thought.

'I ask only one thing of Brandon's wife, dear, and that is that she make him happy. Oh, and that she eventually give me beautiful grandchildren, but that won't be any problem, will it?' Nancie laughed.

So apparently Brandon hadn't confided in his mother about his reason for getting married. Carey hadn't expected him to, of course.

The day passed in a whirl, with a tour of September Hill, a series of rapid decisions on where the ceremony was to be held and how the rooms should be decorated, and the afternoon spent in a host of designer dress shops.

Now and then Carey saw Nancie's eyes rest on her with a speculative gleam. But thank heaven her good manners kept her from demanding an explanation of the fact that just two days ago Carey had claimed to have no plans to marry.

At Donalan's, Carey tried on dozens of dresses, sports outfits, and evening gowns, and Nancie simply stood back and nodded whenever she saw something she approved of. Finally the pile of boxes threatened to swamp Carey, and she protested.

Nancie merely reminded her of the duties she would have as Brandon's hostess, and went off in a corner to talk with Donalan himself while Carey tried to decide on a suitable dress for Lynne as maid of honour. She would much rather have had her best friend, but Gail was out of town. It ought to tickle Brandon's sense of humour, Carey thought, for Lynne to sign their marriage licence, and for the first time she saw something laughable in her engagement.

From Donalan's, they went on to a shoe shop and a boutique which sold lingerie and a jewellery store, and so many others that Carey lost count. But one thing was certain, she concluded at the end of the day as she soaked her weary body in a tub of hot water; there was no doubt whatever about where Brandon Scott had got his administrative style—it had come directly down from his mother.

Carey stood in the middle of the big bedroom on the second floor at September Hill, the bedroom that would be hers from now on. She felt as if it was someone else who stood there in the filmy slip and the white kid shoes, while she herself—the real Carey—watched from a corner. Her hair was almost ready, waiting for the veil to be pinned in place before the last few glossy curls were arranged. Across the big canopied bed lay her wedding gown. True to her word, Nancie had surprised her, for it was Donalan's absolutely-not-for-sale gown. How Nancie had accomplished that feat no one knew, because she would merely smile enigmatically whenever the subject came up.

Lynne was fussing with her hair at the big mirrored dressing table. 'I'm beginning to recognise the advantages of long hair,' she admitted. 'Yours is so pretty today.' She shot a glance at her sister, who hardly seemed to hear. 'Carey, are you all right?'

'What? Oh, I'm fine.'

Lynne took her arm. 'Why don't you sit down a while? You look kind of pale tonight.' Awkwardly, for solicitousness towards her sister was foreign to Lynne, she added, 'Carey, you are happy, aren't you? I mean, you aren't forcing him into this, are you?'

Carey laughed shakily. The thought of anyone forcing Brandon Scott to do anything was ridiculous. She wondered what Lynne would say if she told her that the situation was exactly the opposite. 'No, I'm not forcing him into marrying me, Lynne.'

'You are happy, aren't you? You'd be a fool if you weren't, Carey. Even in my wildest day-dreams, I never considered that this guy would marry anybody.'

'Of course I'm happy.' Carey was aware that she was sounding much like a record stuck in a single groove, but she couldn't do any better today. Certainly she wasn't going to cry on Lynne's shoulder. She supposed it would be a seven-days' wonder for a great many people. Brandon Scott was news any time, but when he married a nobody from his own administrative staff, the tongue that could stay still would be a rare one.

She had only seen him once in nearly a week. Was he afraid she would back out on their bargain? Or was he just giving her a chance to get used to the idea? The day she had seen him, they had ended up in an argument. Perhaps he just didn't want to give her an excuse to break their agreement.

'I was so surprised. Now I know why you were so upset at the idea of my having an affair with him. I won't now, of course.'

'Thanks,' Carey said dryly. That was another positive outcome of this marriage, she told herself. If Lynne had succeeded in drawing Brandon's attention, he would have broken her like a china doll.

'But why didn't you tell me? If I'd known you were engaged to him, I wouldn't have been so worried about that awful necklace.'

'That's nothing to be worried about, ever again,' Carey said flatly.

Lynne looked surprised, but she didn't pursue the subject, asking instead, 'Do you suppose you'll be invited to the White House while you're on your honeymoon? You'll be right in the neighbourhood, and Brandon must know everybody in Washington.'

'I've been to the White House.'

'Hardly in the style Brandon will go in. Though I think it's shabby of him to combine your honeymoon with a business trip. He could have chosen a nicer place than Washington, D.C., too.' Lynne tugged at a curl. 'You'll love his plane, though. I wish I was going. Do you think it will be long before I go back on it?'

'You shouldn't hold your breath, Lynne. You're fortunate to have a job at all.' The girl might just as well know some of the truth now.

'But . . .' Lynne looked horrified.

Nancie came in just then, elegant in a long-sleeved orchid gown that glimmered under the lights. The matching chip hat looked as if it had been made to complement her hair, which, Carey thought, it probably had. She was carrying a florist's box in one hand and a velvet jewel case in the other.

'We may have put this together in just a week, but it's beautiful, Carey,' she said. 'And I think everyone we invited is here. Let's get you into that dress.'

Finally, with the help of Nancie's maid, all of the tiny satin-covered buttons were fastened up the back of the dress, the veil was anchored and the rest of the glossy curls were pinned in place, and Carey stood ready for her wedding.

Nancie fussed with the lace frills and opened the jewel case to hand Carey the delicate cameo pin and earrings that completed the outfit. Carey turned to study her reflection in the full-length mirror, half surprised by how little she looked like herself. The heavy lace-trimmed satin of her dress seemed to be a fog that rose up, threatening to envelope her. She put out a hand, groping for support, and Nancie took it.

'Are you all right, child? Would you like to wait a little while?'

Carey shook her head resolutely. She was in this too

far to back out now, even if she wanted to. With Lynne standing beside her, how could she even want to? She thought about how angry Brandon would be if she refused to go through with this wedding and what form his revenge would take, and she said, 'It's just nerves. I'll be all right.'

'Of course you will,' Nancie said. 'And Clarke will be there to hang on to. I felt the same way on my wedding day—scared out of my mind.' She paused and then added thoughtfully, 'On both my wedding days, come to think of it. Experience doesn't seem to help.'

Carey picked up the single rose that she would carry, and Nancie moved it to the perfect angle so it showed off to best advantage against the pleated satin. 'I'll send Clarke right up,' she promised, with a quick kiss on Carey's cheek.

The waiting was interminable, and Carey looked about the room as if seeing it for the first time. Finally she began to believe that here was where she would be living for the next few months—or years. Already the personal belongings she had left in her apartment were being packed by the movers. No more would she be able to go back to the three rooms she had called home. Now, this was home.

Even her car was up for sale, at Brandon's orders. That was what the shouting match had been about the one time she had seen him in the last week. Carey disliked giving up the freedom that her own car represented, but Brandon was adamant that she would be chauffeured wherever she went, and as always, Brandon's word was law. Carey was still furious.

She looked around at the opulent room, at the pale blue walls, the dark blue carpet so thick that her feet seemed to sink into it, the big canopied bed with side curtains of a fabric so soft and transparent it was like a cobweb, caught back with satin ties that matched the bedspread. On the dressing table were dozens of crystal bottles and jars of cosmetics and perfumes. In the dressing room was a wall of doors concealing more closet space than Carey had ever dreamed of needing. It was a satin prison, she told herself suddenly, a prison for as long as Brandon wanted to keep her there.

Perhaps she could make sure that he would soon be bored and want his freedom, she thought. But she would have to be careful about it, or he would be even angrier and, out of spite, less likely to let her go.

Clarke tapped at the door and came in. When he saw Carey's white face he crossed the room in two steps. 'What's wrong?'

'Nothing.'

'You look as if you'd seen a ghost.' When Carey didn't respond, he continued, 'If this isn't what you want, Carey, I'll take you away. I thought this came up too suddenly to be real. It isn't too late to change your mind.'

'It's much too late,' Carey murmured. Then she caught herself, forced a smile, and said, 'Of course it's what I want, Clarke. It's only nerves. Nancie had them, too, you know.'

He smiled at that and, persuaded, offered his arm. Lynne straightened the chapel train, adjusted the long, trailing veil, and went ahead of them to begin the procession.

I'm drifting out to sea on the fog, Carey thought half coherently as she floated down the stairs. Don't let me be lost, she cried out silently.

Then they were in the big drawing room, fragrant with flowers and warm with the glow of candles. She vaguely heard the string quartet playing a Bach suite, but she couldn't remember which one Nancie had chosen.

She looked up and her eyes were caught and held by Brandon's as he stood across the room. He wasn't mocking now. She hardly knew him, a voice inside her said suddenly, and she was marrying him! Just a business proposition, she reminded herself firmly.

She reached his side, and the clergyman began to speak. Carey heard only bits of the wedding service. She thought it was ironic when the pastor prayed for their lifelong happiness. If the poor man only knew that she had been blackmailed into this marriage, he'd have screamed and run. She heard Brandon's vows, his voice firm and convincing as he promised to love, honour and cherish her until death, and wanted to laugh.

Then the cermony was over, and the guests clustered around them at the altar. Nancie was in tears of happiness; Clarke was so proud that Carey thought it was a miracle he hadn't popped all the buttons off his coat. Lynne was sobbing quietly on David's strong shoulder, possibly because their wedding wouldn't be so exclusive. Carey was finding it hard to maintain any patience with Lynne right now. She studied her own mood and congratulated herself that she was feeling fine, still rather detached as if none of this was happening to her, but otherwise quite at ease.

Brandon took her arm and guided her towards the ballroom where the reception guests were assembled. 'I'm going to start introducing you as the Ice Lady if you don't smile!' he growled in her ear. 'I'm supposed to be quite a catch, you know. Can't you look a little happier?'

'Can't you see I'm just ready to cry, I'm so happy?' Carey said, smiling sweetly up at him.

He muttered something that she didn't hear and pulled her into his arms. One hard forearm held her long veil pressed against the small of her back and Carey couldn't move her head so much as a fraction of an inch. Brandon's other hand caressed the line of her throat as he bent his head slowly towards her.

'Not here,' she whispered.

'Shall we go somewhere else?' he countered. 'I haven't kissed my bride yet—surely I'm allowed that.' His lips moved softly, sensuously over hers, teasing, tasting the softness of her mouth. Then he laughed softly and released her, amused by the anger snapping in her eyes.

Carey heard a spatter of applause from the guests. She glanced around and only then realised that they had been standing in the doorway of the ballroom, in full view of the crowd assembled for the reception.

Damn his timing. 'I wish I'd bitten you,' she muttered.

He looked down at her and smiled indulgently. 'No, you don't,' he said.

CHAPTER FIVE

ONLY a few of the guests in the receiving line made any lasting impression on Carey. One was Mrs Harrison Ayres, who was wearing the famous emerald and amethyst necklace. But mercifully soon Carey had been presented to all of the guests, the wedding dinner was served, the enormous cake was cut, and the newly married couple were toasted in champagne.

They were just raising their glasses to drink when the brilliant flash went off in their faces. Carey was startled, but Brandon, who had much more experience with pursuing photographers, identified the light instantly. At a gesture from him, two waiters appeared beside the offending young man and, one at each elbow, started to hustle him out of the room. He shook them off with an air, straightened his jacket, and said over his shoulder, 'Wouldn't you like to know how I got in, Mr Scott?'

Brandon laughed. 'As a matter of fact, I would,' he said. The young man breezed across the room to the head table.

'I'll tell you, if I can stay through the reception,' he bargained.

'You'll tell my security chief, and you won't stay,' Brandon countered. 'You should know better than to try to make a deal with me. And you should also know better than to use flash lighting when you don't want to be discovered.'

'I know,' the young man said sadly. 'It went off by mistake, or you'd have never known I was here. I'd taken a dozen pictures before that.'

Brandon's eyes narrowed.

'I'd like a couple of shots of the dancing,' the young man wheedled. 'I'm only trying to make a living.'

Carey sipped her champagne. 'Self-confidence should

be rewarded,' she pointed out calmly.

'The lady wants you to stay,' Brandon said. 'But don't make any sudden moves.'

The young man beamed. 'Thanks, Mrs Scott!' He was gone into the crowd in an instant.

'Something tells me he'll be back,' Brandon muttered. 'The orchestra is waiting for us.'

He swept Carey around the floor in the first waltz, then handed her over to Clarke. After the two mandatory dances, Carey found that she couldn't take three steps without another man cutting in.

Once she looked up into Doug Mason's eyes.

'You're coming up in the world, aren't you?' he said sarcastically. 'I thought the last time I heard you mention Brandon Scott's name he was still less than the dust beneath your feet. But I guess you got what you were holding out for, didn't you?'

'Doug, I'm sorry I didn't tell you myself. I should have, I know, and I understand why you're hurt.'

'I don't think you understand much of anything. I was really being dense that day, wasn't I, when it didn't dawn on me what was going on? I still can't decide if you were really upset or just hysterical with delight over your triumph. But I wish you hadn't picked on me to get you home. I didn't know I was consoling the boss's fiancée until I landed on the carpet in his office.'

Before Carey could question further, Brandon tapped on Doug's shoulder, and it was too late to say anything at all.

After such a variety of dancers, it was heaven to circle the floor with Brandon, to be held so firmly, to feel that each step was perfectly in order. She looked up to find his eyes fixed on her with a peculiar brooding intensity. Was he already regretting this rash marriage? Frankly, she hoped so. Her first taste of what life would be like as his wife was enough to scare anyone.

Suddenly her feet refused to move any more. 'I'd like to sit down for a little while, please, Brandon.' She held out a hand. It was shaking.

'Of course. You've danced every dance; I should have realised.' He signalled a waiter to bring her a glass of champagne. 'Did you know that's the first time you've ever used my name? It's always been Mr Scott before.'

'Oh—has it?'

'You know darned well it has.' He took the glass from the silver tray the waiter offered and handed it to her.

'I guess I'll get used to it.'

'You'd better. It would be a little embarrassing if you slipped into old habits at a dinner party.'

Nancie came up to them. 'Are you two ready to dance the last waltz?' she asked. 'A few people have left already, but most of them are just waiting for Carey to throw her bouquet.'

'My one bedraggled rose, you mean?' Carey asked. 'Is it really so late?'

'Not really. But you shouldn't have to be entertaining a crowd tonight, anyway.'

Brandon laughed. 'Would you like to explain that comment, Mother?'

'I merely meant that you have a long day tomorrow,' Nancie said, refusing to allow her poise to be shattered. 'I'll never again want to play hostess at September Hill— but I'm stuck with it tonight.'

'And you're welcome to the job!' Carey told her.

No one else intruded on their waltz. It was just them and the music and the soft lights playing over the polished floor. Their steps matched perfectly.

A really good dancer, Carey was thinking, is hard to find. Especially when a man was as tall and as powerfully built as Brandon was, it was unusual for him to move so gracefully.

Then the music ended, and she found herself at the foot of the staircase. They walked up the first flight, and all the unmarried women gathered in the hall. Carey aimed her rose straight at Lynne, but in between them another girl stretched out a hand and caught the flower.

At the door to her sitting room, Carey hesitated, but

Brandon pushed the door open and followed her in. 'Our guests, and especially my mother, would hardly expect us to go to opposite ends of the house while they're still here,' he pointed out. He sat down in one of the velvet chairs, looking perfectly comfortable in his formal clothes. The white waistcoat and tie emphasised his tan. He looked up at her inquiringly.

Embarrassed at being caught staring, Carey moved nervously across the room to a mirror and took off her earrings. 'I didn't have a chance to say thank you for these, Brandon. They're lovely.'

'They suit you,' he said, leaving her wondering what that meant. He rose and walked across to the window seat, with its piled cushions and built-in bookshelves. He pulled the books off one of the shelves, spun a dial, and opened a small safe that had been hidden there.

'How clever!'

'It's probably the first place a burglar would look,' Brandon said dryly. 'But it's convenient. I'll write the combination down for you.' He took out another velvet case. 'Here is the rest of the groom's gift to the bride. Mother thought it would be too much with your dress.'

Carey opened the case and stared down at the soft glow of a double strand of pearls. 'It's beautiful!' she breathed.

'My wife will always have the best,' he said quietly.

Carey felt as though she had been slapped. He didn't need to make it so painfully obvious that the jewels, the whole show, weren't for her but for the position of Mrs Brandon Scott—whoever that should happen to be.

'I see. I'll wear them whenever you want someone reminded that you have a wife.'

'You'll wear them tonight, after the guests are gone. We'll be going back downstairs.'

'Perhaps I should have asked: Are the pearls mine, or do I leave them behind for the next Mrs Scott?'

'They're yours—do as you like with them. Give them to the Salvation Army, for all I care.' He sounded bored.

'Of course. It would be gauche for Mrs Brandon Scott

to have second-hand anything—except, possibly, a second-hand husband.'

'If you think being bitchy is going to get you out of this any earlier, I suggest your reconsider.' He stood up abruptly. 'Wear the pearls.'

Her eyes locked angrily with his and as always it was hers that fell first. She would wear the pearls, as she would do whatever he told her to do, because if she didn't Lynne would suffer.

It really wasn't very smart of you to allow him to catch you in an open-ended threat, Carey told herself. She would never be totally free, even if he decided to let her go, as long as Lynne was at Universal. He could always hurt Lynne, and he knew that would hurt Carey.

Well, she would encourage Lynne to move on, and that would lessen the threat. In the meantime, she could always hope that Brandon would soon become bored. After all, she was scarcely the kind of woman he was usually seen with. Surely there were things she could do to hasten that decision?

Suddenly she became aware of his fiery brown eyes fixed on her. 'And don't start planning a way out,' he suggested harshly. 'It won't be easy. You'll get no short-cuts from me.'

'I won't do anything that will endanger my sister.'

'Well, you just remember little Lynne and her sticky fingers.'

'Lynne did not take that necklace!'

Brandon's gaze was almost unreadable, but Carey thought she saw a gleam of pity in his velvet eyes. Then he said, 'The staff will be serving a light supper when the guests have gone.'

'I'm not hungry.'

'You should be—you ate scarcely anything at dinner.'

She was surprised that he had noticed. 'They needn't bother for my sake.'

Brandon started towards his own bedroom, pulling his white tie loose. 'Supper will be served in half an hour, and you will come down, dressed in something more appropriate than that thing you're wearing, even if I have to dress you myself.' The door didn't quite slam behind him.

Carey's eyes were still burning with tears half an hour later as she came downstairs. In the pier mirror at the turn of the stairway she caught a glimpse of herself in the dusty-rose dress, with her shoulders almost bare and the pearls gleaming softly at her throat. She had had trouble subduing a shiver when Nancie's maid had put the necklace on. She wondered if this dress would please Brandon. She doubted it; if he thought of a Donalan one-of-a-kind as 'that thing you're wearing'—as though she had picked it up in a bargain basement—how could anything else please him? She began to wonder just how she was to make it through the meal, and the two or three years yet to come was an unbearable thought.

He was standing before the fireplace, one elbow on the mantel, watching the flickering embers. As she came in he glanced at his wristwatch and remarked, 'You're on time to the moment.'

Carey, stung, retorted, 'I've never been late in my life, and I don't intend to start now, regardless of the circumstances.'

He merely raised an eyebrow. 'Would you like a drink?'

'No, thank you. I had plenty of champagne.'

'Do you mind if I do?'

'Of course not. Whether you pickle your liver or not isn't any concern of mine.'

Brandon stopped in the act of pouring Scotch and then deliberately filled the glass. 'Don't tell me you're going to turn into a temperance advocate.'

'What you do doesn't matter to me. Perhaps you'll die, and I'll be a wealthy widow.'

'I wondered when you would start considering all the advantages of marrying money.'

'I'm sorry to disappoint you by taking so long. It has so many disadvantages, you see.'

Just then the butler, Whitney, announced that supper was served. Brandon drained his glass, set it aside, and offered his arm in an exaggerated gesture.

Carey could never remember what she ate that night, if indeed she ate anything at all. The conversation flashed back and forth, never sarcastic or rude, because all the time Whitney was there right behind her chair, responding to the slightest signal, but under the surface of their voices lurked a sneer. Carey rather enjoyed it; she knew that whatever she said Brandon could not retaliate as he would like.

The only thing that she remembered clearly was her feeling that it was absurd for the two of them to use the formal table in the dining room when it was intended to seat at least twelve. One almost had to shout from end to end. On the other hand, she told herself, at least Brandon hadn't opted for an intimate meal served in her sitting room. Surely that would have been more appropriate for a wedding night!

She concealed the sardonic humour she felt as she watched him drain his wine-glass and refill it. Regardless of what he said, he must be feeling a little regret, or he wouldn't be drinking so much. At least that was the reason she was giving herself for the wine she was drinking—which was also too much, she knew.

When she declined dessert and coffee, Brandon said, 'It's late. Why don't you go on up? We're leaving early tomorrow, you know.'

'I think I will. It's been a long day.'

As she left the room, she saw him refill his brandy glass.

Nancie's maid was waiting for her in the big bedroom. Neither spoke until the dusty-rose dress was hung up and Carey, wearing a dark green lace negligee over a low-cut satin gown, was sitting before the mirror as the maid brushed her hair.

'Madam was lovely today,' the maid said. 'There were many comments about you and your gown.'

'Thank you.' Carey had been longing for a chance to

ask the maid how Nancie had obtained the dress from
Donalan', but it didn't seem to matter any more.

'I've already arranged for the gown to be taken to the
cleaners,' the maid said. 'Then when it is returned, I'll
pack it away so that it will be ready for Madam's
daughters to use.'

More likely the second Mrs Scott, Carey thought. She
wished fretfully that everyone would stop assuming that
there would be children from this marriage. It would
have been thoughtful of Brandon to have at least told his
mother not to get in any hurry for her beautiful grandchildren.

The maid coiled Carey's hair into a snood so that it
would not tangle as she slept and put the brushes away.
'Madam will be happy to have her own maid when she
returns,' the woman said.

Probably not happy, Carey decided, but I'll adjust.
And I hope I can stop her from calling me madam, and
referring to me as if I'm not here. 'It will take me some
time to get used to having a maid. Mrs Dennis is taking
care of that, too.'

'Mrs Dennis is delighted to have a daughter-in-law,'
the maid said wisely. 'It has been a pleasure to take care
of a very young lady again.'

Carey crushed the desire to say, 'I am not a child!'

The maid turned off all but the bedside light and said,
'Just ring if you need anything, madam.'

Carey yawned and got into bed as soon as the woman
had left the room. But — as she had half expected —
she couldn't sleep. She tossed for a few minutes without
being able to find a comfortable position, then got up to
hunt in her handbag for a sleeping pill. 'Unusual thing to
be wanting on a honeymoon,' she told herself wryly.

She climbed back into bed, swallowed the capsule, and
popped the lid back on to the bottle, setting it on the
bedside table. She had just flicked the lamp off when the
door from her sitting room opened and Brandon came
in.

She sat up straight. 'What are you doing here?'

'I should have thought it would be obvious to you. It is our wedding night—remember?'

'Oh, no.'

Brandon came across the room and sat down on the edge of the bed. He was wearing a brown velour dressing gown with a wide collar that revealed his tanned chest. He raised a hand and brushed a wisp of hair back from her cheek.

Carey felt the blood pounding in her ears. 'But you said you weren't interested in going to bed with me,' she said, her voice small and breathless. 'You said . . .'

'I didn't say anything of the sort. You assumed that because I didn't take you up on your offer that day in my office that I wasn't interested. Carey, my dear, why does a man in my position marry at all unless he wants an heir?'

'Oh, my God . . .' Her voice trailed off. Her mind was frantically playing back everything that he had said on that fatal day. He was right, she was forced to conclude; at no time had he said she would not be expected to perform all of a wife's duties. He just hadn't spelled it out that he intended to share her bed. The treacherous sneak, she thought. How could she have been so dumb?

He let a finger slide gently down her throat. 'You're a beautiful woman, Carey, and you piqued my interest the day you turned me down. Very few women have done that, and you did it in a way that made me determined to have you. Since that day on the rooftop I've wanted to light a fire in you that would melt you for ever.'

'Revenge? Because I didn't want to play house?' Her voice was little more than a hoarse whisper.

'The name doesn't matter.'

'Why go to such a length? Why marry me? I offered to go to bed with you, if that was what you wanted.'

He shook his head. 'Oh, no, Carey, my proud beauty. That wouldn't have done at all. I wasn't about to give up my hold on you for a one-night stand, when I could have so much more. Now you'll be right here—for as long as I want you.'

She swallowed hard. Her mind was spinning a little from the wine she had drunk and the sleeping pill beginning to take effect. 'But you said a housekeeper . . . you wanted a hostess . . .'

He smiled. 'Carey, you're grasping at straws. You disappoint me. I have a housekeeper—you've met Mrs Whitney. It's easy enough to find a hostess, and easier still to convince a lady to share my bed. But I'm thirty-four, and at that age, a man begins to think an empire isn't worth building unless he has a son to leave it to. I don't want to be tangled up in the usual marriage, but neither is anyone going to question the parentage of my child. And even if I tire of you, you'll leave here alone.'

'My God, you can't be serious! Do you actually want a baby to be born of this hate?'

'You won't hate me, Carey.' His voice was a husky promise. 'I'll teach you to delight in every instant of our lovemaking. And how could a child of ours turn out badly? Look at the potential!'

Carey was speechless.

'Do you know, I've always wanted to see you with your hair down?' he mused. 'It was as much as I could do today to keep my hands out of your hair.' He reached for the snood, pulling it off to release the soft, shiny mass. It fell forward over her shoulders as Carey tried to hide her face. 'Beautiful,' he murmured, and raised a handful of glossy curls to his lips.

Carey, in a last frantic bid for freedom, pushed the sheet aside and scrambled to escape from the bed.

He let her hair slide through his fingers, but stopped her easily, one hand locking on to her wrist, the other arm closing about her waist. His hand caressed her silky skin as he drew her slowly, inexorably back on to the bed.

Carey fought him, lashing out with her fists and trying to kick. But her struggles seemed to amuse him, and she succeeded only in loosening the belt on his robe until his chest was bare and warm against her, the dark hairs curling crisply against her fingertips.

He let her struggle until she lay panting and exhausted. 'All worn out?' he asked then, and she lashed out again.

Slowly, without apparent effort, he drew her hands above her head and pinned her wrists there, her arms helpless at full length. With his other hand he untied the narrow ribbons that held her gown together, and an instant later his hand gently cupped her breast and his mouth teased the nipple to an excited peak.

'All right, you've proved you're stronger than I am,' Carey spat. 'What's next? Rape?'

'Oh, no. I'm not going to descend to rape—I won't have to. I'm just going to give you a lesson in how to purr, little kitten.'

'I'll never purr for you!'

'Never is a very long time,' he said softly against her lips.

She turned her head to avoid his kiss, but he merely said, 'Stubborn, aren't you?' and directed his attention to the soft skin of her throat and the sensitive triangle just under her ear.

Carey shivered as his teeth gently tugged at her earlobe. She was feeling dizzy, the combined effects of the wine, the champagne, and the sleeping pill. Why had she drunk so much wine at dinner? she asked herself angrily, and shivered again as Brandon's hand returned to cup her breast. A tiny dart of pleasure ran through her at his gentleness, and she turned her head to stare into his eyes, wondering what emotions might lie in their depths. But in the darkened room, she could not see—in the instant before his mouth descended to claim hers—what he might be thinking.

She had thought his kiss there on the rooftop arousing, but it was a firecracker compared to the dynamite that exploded in her now. He smiled at her response, and grew more demanding, the flame of his desire fed by her surrender, until the conflagration consumed them both.

*   *   *

Carey stirred, luxuriating for an instant in the slickness of satin sheets sliding over her bare skin and the warmth of the hand massaging her back. Not since she was a child had anyone awakened her by rubbing her back, and for an instant Carey drowsily thought it was her mother sitting on the edge of her bed and waking her for school. Then she opened her eyes to see the telephone and the bottle of sleeping pills on the bedside table, and she remembered where she was. She jerked away from that warm hand and spat, 'Keep your filthy hands off me!'

Brandon raised an eyebrow, sat up, and punched his pillow into shape. He sank back into it and said softly, 'That's funny. I don't remember you saying much about that last night after a certain point.'

'Last night I had far too much to drink.' Carey slid out of bed, reaching for her negligee on the floor. She glanced fearfully over her shoulder, but Brandon didn't seem interested in stopping her. He was, however, watching her with a good deal of appreciation. She shrugged into the lace robe and said, 'If I hadn't combined all that wine with a sleeping pill, last night would never have happened.'

'Would you care to bet on that?' He sounded only mildly interested.

'I'll tell you something right now—there is no way that it will ever be repeated. You will never seduce me again.' She flounced across the room to the dressing table and seized her hairbrush. 'A man who has to trick a woman into marrying him and then use force on their wedding night, isn't much of a man at all.'

Brandon drew a short, sharp breath.

Carey yanked the brush through her hair, shuddering inwardly at what she had said. That kind of attack might get almost any kind of response.

But he laughed, a short, humourless laugh. 'Another of your unexpected talents, Carey. You can take the sunshine out of anybody's day.' He got out of bed and tied the belt of his robe with short, savage movements.

'But you do have a point. I don't plan to try any more seduction on you. I learned a long time ago when to cut my losses.'

'Are you going to let me go?' Carey asked eagerly.

'You don't think it will be that easy, do you?' he taunted. 'No. But the next time, you'll beg me to make love to you.'

Carey laughed. 'You do have a high opinion of yourself, don't you? If you're waiting for an invitation, you'll wait for a long time. What about our trip, by the way?'

'Our honeymoon?' he mocked. 'We're going through with it. Mostly because I still have business to conduct. And you don't really think I'd leave my bride behind, do you? I'm smarter than that.'

'And you really mean that you won't bother me any more?'

'Of course I mean it, although you'll change your mind very soon,' he promised. The door clicked shut behind him.

Carey yanked the brush mercilessly through her tangled hair till tears came to her eyes. Somehow, she thought, he would get the better of that bargain too.

Carey smothered a yawn and sneaked a look at her wristwatch. No, dinner wasn't dragging; it just seemed as it they had been sitting here for ever. Washington was foggy and damp and boring, and Carey was miserable. The days weren't so bad; she shopped and toured the city. It wasn't as much fun as it had been in the days when a group of girls had laid over between flights, but it would do. At least during the day Brandon was in business meetings and she never saw him.

But in the evenings she had to play the loving bride. Almost every evening they had been invited out. They had been to Congressional cocktail parties, private dinners, embassy dances; things that a few weeks ago would have been exciting were now dull to the point of tedium. Tonight they were alone, and it was even worse. They had exchanged scarcely a word beyond discussing

the menu in monosyllables. It had been the longest week
of Carey's life.

She had no idea how long the charade would last;
Brandon had given no indication of how long his
business might take, and she was in no position to ask.
Nor did she want to let him know that she was tired of the
way things were. She certainly didn't want to do anything that he might interpret as an invitation to change
their way of life.

At least he had kept to his promise; their suite had two
bedrooms and he had never come near her. She was
beginning to think that he had meant what he said, that
his pride would not allow him to approach her again. She
didn't know if he was seeing other women; he certainly
had the opportunity, and Washington was full of interesting women. If he was, she was glad. Surely some day
soon he would tire of this and realise that she was not
going to give in.

'Would you care to dance?'

'No, thank you.' It seemed they couldn't even dance
comfortably together any more, and Carey had started
turning down all invitations.

Brandon stared moodily across the room.

Carey smiled to herself. This was obviously not a
pleasant way for him to spend an evening, either. Surely
this torture wouldn't continue for ever.

'Brandon, darling, how I've been longing to run into
you!'

Carey looked up at the owner of the cheery voice. A
more beautiful woman she had never seen; Michelle
Lantry was even more stunning in person than on a
magazine cover.

Brandon was on his feet. 'Michelle! What a pleasant
surprise!'

He needn't sound so damned enthusiastic about it,
Carey thought. After all, it was his own fault that he was
stuck in this distasteful situation.

'Oh, come on, Bran, you can't have forgotten that I
was here doing that magazine layout. And I know where

you hang out, so it was only a matter of time. Even if you didn't get around to calling me.' The model's voice was arch.

'I've been tempted,' Brandon smiled. Carey could have stabbed him with a steak knife. He needn't be so obvious about how bored he was with her, she thought. 'Michelle, I'd like you to meet Carey.'

'Ah, yes, the little wife.' Michelle's eyes raked over Carey and obviously found her lacking. Then she gestured to the man who stood behind her. 'And this is Elliott Lang, who's studying here,' she added carelessly.

Elliot held Carey's hand for a long moment. 'Lovely,' he said, looking into her eyes. 'Just lovely.'

'Don't mind Elliot,' Michelle advised coolly. 'He was in Paris for a year before he came here. The French influence hasn't worn off entirely yet; I wouldn't want you to get the wrong idea, Carey.' She looked Carey over again and dismissed her. 'Bran, darling, do come and dance with me and tell me everything I've been missing back home. I'll be going home in a few days, and I want to be current on all of the gossip.'

Brandon murmured an excuse to Carey—she was amazed that he had even remembered she was there— and followed Michelle out to the dance floor as meekly as a puppy.

'Are they good friends?' Elliot pulled out a chair. 'May I sit down?'

'They're very good friends, as the saying goes.' Carey wondered for a moment about the rumour that had hinted at a marriage between them. Michelle hadn't seemed concerned about meeting Brandon's wife. Of course, she hadn't let it stop her from taking him out to dance as though she had a leash on him, either. Michelle probably knew all about Brandon's occasional interesting women, and she probably didn't care. Perhaps she was simply confident that he would come back to her eventually. They'd make a good pair, Carey reflected.

Elliot interrupted her thoughts. 'How long have you been married?'

'Just about a week.'

'That explains it,' he sighed. 'I thought I was beginning to lose my touch when you went off in a daze like that.'

Carey laughed—it was the first time she had seen anything to laugh about in a week.

'That's better. I don't want to be familiar, but I didn't catch your last name.'

'Scott. But please call me Carey.' She hated to be reminded that she now shared Brandon's name.

'I'm honoured. But I'm also surprised. You're honeymooning in Washington, D.C.?' His tone was incredulous.

'Brandon's combining it with a business trip.'

'That explains it. And you're sightseeing while he's lobbying Congress? How exciting.'

'What makes you think he's lobbying?'

'Everybody in this city wants something from a senator or a representative. Or the President, perhaps. Nobody comes here for fun; it's far too humid even at this season, and really not a comfortable city at all. So what are you doing to occupy your time?'

'I really can't get excited about the tourist attractions. I am doing some research on my family tree, though. I'm hoping the Library of Congress will have what I need.'

'What information are you looking for?'

'My great-grandparents immigrated, and they would never say much about why they chose to leave England.'

'And you think you have a black sheep? Are you certain you want to find out? The reasons may not have been pleasant ones.' He didn't wait for an answer. 'The British Embassy might be of some help. I'll call a friend I have there and ask him, and we'll go looking tomorrow morning. With two of us, we should find something in half the time.'

'I'd be happy to have help, but I don't think you'll find my old family records fascinating.'

Elliot flashed a smile. 'Of course not, but if I break my neck finding your records, you can't refuse to have lunch with me, and that I'd find fascinating.' He looked out towards the dance floor. 'That is, if your husband doesn't object.'

Carey followed his glance, seeing Brandon and Michelle in the middle of the floor, dancing very close together, apparently absorbed in each other. 'I can't see what he could object to,' she said steadily. 'How did you meet Michelle?'

'Oh, I play around with a camera now and then, so whenever I get a chance I watch the professionals at work. I met Michelle at the Lincoln Memorial when she was sitting on Honest Abe's lap wearing a very skimpy bikini.'

'I hope the film was ruined.'

'I think that one was strictly for fun. In any case, it was a little cold for the bikini, and the goosepimples probably ruined it. I don't know why she picked me up, unless her ego is flattered by having someone my age following her around. Or perhaps it's that she just can't stand to be unescorted. Have you ever noticed that models are never by themselves?'

'You sound very relaxed about it.'

'I am. Michelle's fun to have around sometimes, thought she's not really my type. But who knows—she might be a valuable connection some day.'

Apparently she was Brandon's type, however, for when they returned to the table he was smiling and looking ten years younger.

Michelle and Elliot stayed only a few moments longer. When Michelle swept out, Elliot hung back and asked Carey, 'Is nine all right tomorrow morning, in the hotel lobby? You are staying here, aren't you?'

'Yes, I'll be there,' Carey promised.

'Where are you going?' Brandon asked, frowning again. 'Sightseeing with the whippersnapper?'

'As a matter of fact, no. We're going to the census and records places to dig out information on my family.'

'I didn't know you were interested in genealogy.'

'But then you really don't know much about me at all,'

Carey snapped, and could have bitten her tongue off. Why rock the boat?

'Is that an invitation for me to start learning?' He looked faintly interested.

She stared through him.

They were silent all the way to their suite. As Carey started for her bedroom, though, Brandon stopped her. 'Be careful in playing around with the Lang boy,' he warned.

'Are you concerned that I might take him away from Michelle?'

'Of course not. But you might give him ideas, and he could easily get out of control.'

'I don't remember encouraging you at all, and you certainly got out of control,' Carey remarked. 'I didn't realise that being married meant that I wasn't allowed to speak to any other man.'

'I can't imagine you living up to that promise, either,' Brandon said coldly, and went to his own room.

'Well, Carey,' she told herself, 'it looks as if you finally got the best of an argument.'

CHAPTER SIX

'CHAMPAGNE!' Elliot told the waiter grandly. 'We have something to celebrate, after all.'

Carey giggled. 'Is finding a great-great-grandparent something to celebrate?'

'It makes a good excuse, doesn't it?'

'Well, yes. I always did suspect my family had noble connections. My father would have made a great eighteenth-century playboy; he must have been a throw-back to someone.'

The champagne arrived, and Elliot took a sip before saying, 'If that was all you wanted to know, I could have saved us all the dusty old books and miles of microfilm.'

'Really? How?'

He reached across the table for her hand. 'Look at this—the long fingers and the lovely shape. There has to be at least a duke in your family tree. Maybe even a royal prince, but I'm afraid that would have been on the wrong side of the blanket.'

'How wonderful it would be to be almost a princess!'

'You are a princess to me,' Elliot said softly, and raised her hand to his lips. As he put it down gently and toasted her with his champagne glass, she looked up to find Brandon staring at her from a table two rows away.

Elliot saw her expression. 'Did the husband show up? I can see I'm going to have to hire a hit man to take care of him—he's ruining all my fun.'

'I don't think that would be a good idea.'

'I'll think of something—I'm not going to let him keep upsetting my digestion. Drink up, Princess. Let's get a little tippled and go look for a square corner in the Pentagon.'

'That doesn't sound like much fun.' But she obedi-ently drank her champagne.

'I know. That's why you have to be snozzled to enjoy the experience.'

Carey giggled, and, suddenly reckless, allowed him to refill her glass. She hadn't had so much carefree fun in a year. Elliot was a charming companion, so much different from the men she had dated in the last months. While she was sure that she could never think of Elliot as any more than a friend with a sparkling personality, she saw no harm in enjoying their time together.

The afternoon passed in a glow of laughter. She was still laughing as she walked into the hotel suite that afternoon, with, she estimated, an hour before Brandon would arrive. Instead, she was startled to find him waiting, his back against the mantel, wristwatch in hand.

'You're late. It must have been an interesting afternoon,' he said curtly and strapped his watch back on his wrist.

Carey giggled, remembering. 'Oh, yes, it was.' She sat down, unhooked the strap of her high-heeled sandal, and slid the shoe painfully off. 'I must have walked miles today.'

'Was that the best entertainment Elliot could come up with? Or was that all you would agree to?'

Carey slid the other sandal off and looked up at him in surprise. 'For heaven's sake, Brandon, you sound jealous.'

'You're not worth being jealous over. But you did promise to be faithful; I was just concerned about whether you were being so. It would be considerate of you to keep your marriage vows at least until the honeymoon is over.'

'Are you keeping yours?' she countered, and continued thoughtfully, massaging a slim foot as she spoke, 'Did I promise that? I don't remember promising anything of the sort.'

'It was in the marriage ceremony, right along with love and honour.'

'Oh, then! I was in such a fog right then that I hardly remember anything at all. Surely I can't be held

responsible for a promise I don't remember making.'
She started for her bedroom. 'I'd better dress for dinner.
I won't keep you waiting long.'

Before she had taken three steps, Brandon seized her
arm in a painfully tight grip and swung her around to face
him. Without her shoes, Carey had to tip her head back
to look up at his face, which was dark with anger. She felt
tiny beside him, powerless in his grasp.

'You're hurting me, Brandon!'

'Do you really expect me to let you get away with this?
To let you dance around under my nose with your little
friend panting after you, and then to stand by quietly
while you dismiss me? I'm not a sharing man, Carey. I'd
have thought you would have learned that by now.'

She said, a bit breathlessly, 'What's the matter? Are
you frustrated because I haven't begged you to come
back to my bed? Are you angry because I'm immune to
your charms?'

He pulled her so close that Carey could feel his heart
pounding against her breasts. She tried to turn her face
away, but he captured her chin in one strong hand and
forced her to look at him.

'You will give me that invitation, and it will be soon,'
he promised, his lips almost against hers. 'But all I want
right now is what you gave Elliot quite willingly—a kiss.'

She hadn't allowed Elliot to kiss her, but Carey was
darned if she'd admit it. And she wasn't going to give in
to this sort of treatment. She would not allow him to
manhandle her like this. 'No,' she said.

Brandon's eyes hardened. 'Then, if you won't give it
to me, I'll just take it.'

It was a brutal kiss, punishing, bruising her mouth,
grinding her lips against her teeth. He held her so tightly
that she couldn't move, one large hand twisted into her
hair so she couldn't pull away, cradling the back of her
head to hold her mouth against his. Carey's fists
pounded ineffectually on his shoulders, and Brandon
didn't seem to notice that she was striking him. He
merely pulled her even closer, moulding her body

against him, his kiss forcing her mouth open.

Then Carey bit him.

He swore and let go of her, his hand catching in the long strands of her hair as it tumbled down. She stood up straight, tossing her head defiantly, tears in her eyes from the pain in her abused scalp and her bruised mouth. 'I'm waiting for an apology, Brandon,' she said fiercely.

'I hope you're prepared for a long wait.' He turned to the bar and pulled the stopper out of a decanter.

Carey mustered all the dignity she could summon, to allow her to walk across the room instead of fleeing like a frightened rabbit. Common sense told her that he wouldn't follow her, but it took all of her willpower to keep from locking the bedroom door once she had reached sanctuary. To run from him, or to lock the door, would be to admit that she was afraid of him, and Carey's stiff backbone could never allow that.

When she came out a few minutes later, her poise regained and the bruises on her mouth covered with lipstick, a waiter was putting the finishing touches on a table for two by the window. She waited until he had gone before asking Brandon, 'Why the intimate meal? Are you afraid I'll go running to Elliot to complain that you're treating me badly?'

'It seemed prudent to make sure you were sober before we went downstairs,' Brandon said smoothly. 'I'm sure you didn't stop with the champagne at lunch.'

'Oh, I'm perfectly sober. The high I was on is of a different kind. It's called being happy.' She settled herself at the table. 'But then I shouldn't expect you to recognise my mood. After all, you've never seen me happy before. And you're not likely to have the opportunity in the future.'

'I've always wondered,' Brandon mused, 'why so many married men go to the trouble of keeping a mistress—now I know. Have a hotel maid pack for you tomorrow morning—we'll be checking out in the afternoon.'

'What a shame. I've just started to enjoy myself.'

Carey sampled her prime rib and asked curiously, 'Are we going home because you're concerned that Elliot might actually become my lover, or is it that you can't stand for anyone to be laughing at you behind your back?'

Brandon frowned. 'Elliot or no Elliot, we're leaving tomorrow. My business is finished, and I need to get back to the main office.'

'Of course,' Carey said soothingly. But she didn't believe a word of it, and she made no effort to hide her doubt.

Two hours later she and Elliot were watching the dancers. Brandon and Michelle were again on the dance floor, this time staying off to the edge where they were less conspicuous. Elliot sighed and said, 'And he's taking you home? Just like that?'

'We leave tomorrow.'

'So much for your tour of the White House on Thursday.'

'I imagine the First Lady will survive the disappointment,' Carey mocked.

'I'll have to call her and tell her to cancel tea.' He distractedly started patting his pockets. 'I hope it's not too late; she was planning to invite all her special friends to meet you. I've got her unlisted number here somewhere . . .'

He sounded so serious that Carey burst out laughing. 'You needn't worry about my disappointment, Elliot,' she teased. 'I didn't vote for her husband anyway.'

He rewarded her with a grin, then sobered abruptly. 'What's the matter with that man anyway? Doesn't he want to let you have any fun?'

'Not unless it's his kind of fun.'

'Is he jealous or something?'

'He might be, but he would never admit it.'

'I can't see what he'd be jealous of, anyway. He's the one who gets to run his fingers through that gorgeous hair. You wouldn't let me do that in a million years.' He reached for a chestnut curl which lay loose across her shoulder.

'No, Elliot.' Carey pulled away.

'See what I mean? What's his problem? He's making time with Michelle . . .'

Carey shrugged it off. 'What do I care what he does, as long as he leaves me alone?' She put a hand thoughtfully to her bruised lip.

Elliot looked horrified. 'And you've been married a whole week? Family life really is going to hell in the States, isn't it?' He sipped his drink. 'Since he's got Michelle, why don't you take a lover back with you and see what happens?'

'I wouldn't know how to interview the applicants, unless you'd be interested, Elliot. Are your fees reasonable?'

He acted hurt. 'For you, Princess, never a fee.'

'Do you mean it? You wouldn't charge me at all?'

'Well—only my expenses. And I have to warn you, I am expensive.'

'Sorry. That's the sort of thing that got me into all this trouble. I'm tired of talking, Elliot. Let's go dance and enjoy this last evening.

One thing Carey had to admit; all of Brandon's employees were well-trained. She surveyed the assortment of fruit, magazines, pillows—everything for the air traveller's comfort—that surrounded her chair in the common room of the big jet. Not only didn't they forget anything, but they immediately faded into the woodwork when their tasks were completed.

Brandon came out of the little side room he used as a flying office and sat down across from her. He surveyed her with brooding eyes for several minutes.

Carey tossed her magazine down and snapped, 'Haven't you ever seen me before?'

'Oh, stop being bitchy. I know you're trying to enjoy complaining, but you can't really like listening to yourself.'

Carey was silent. He had hit that one on the head.

Despite the way she had sounded for the last week, it really didn't come naturally. He certainly brought out the worst in her, but she smiled sweetly and said, 'So divorce me and let me worry about how I turn out.'

'I've been doing some thinking about us,' he said.

'And what conclusions have you come to?'

'If you expect me to say I've decided it can't work and to throw myself at your feet with apologies and a divorce decree, you'd better change your expectations. I'm willing to admit, between us, that I shouldn't have left anything unsaid. I should have made it plain that I expected you to be a wife in the bedroom too.'

'That's big of you.' Carey sounded only vaguely interested as she looked over the fruit in the bowl, selected a Golden Delicious apple, and took a bite. 'Just think, if you'd been wise enough to stay out of my room that night, we could have had a nice quiet annulment. Now it will have to be a sloppy divorce.'

'Why don't we both just forget what happened that night?'

She thoughtfully took another bite out of the apple. 'Why? Did Superlover get a bad review?'

He glared at her. 'In case you're tempted to try some foolish stunt that you think will convince me to divorce you—don't.'

'A foolish stunt compared to what?' Carey asked interestedly. 'On a scale of foolish, I couldn't possibly outdo the situation I'm in now. Of course, I think it's a little foolish of you to persist in this nonsense.'

'You're only delaying things, you know. The longer you fuel my resentment, the longer it will be before you have your freedom.'

Carey shrugged. 'That's a double-edged sword, you know.'

'Perhaps. I think we'll see whom it injures first. Now, you may not have agreed to sleep with me . . .'

'And I haven't seen anything that tempts me to change my mind, either,' Carey inserted conversationally.

He ignored the interruption. 'But you did promise to

make my home a pleasant, peaceful place. That promise you weren't tricked into—it was made very plain. Now would you at least live up to that bargain?'

Carey was silent. Finally she said, 'All right. I did promise you a well-run home—thank you for reminding me of it! I trust I get a peaceful bedroom in return? No more tricks?'

'Until you decide to invite me in.'

Carey's smile was tight. 'Don't hold your breath.'

'I'm not—I'm absolutely certain of the outcome. Do we have a deal?' He held out a hand.

She shook her head. 'I'm not making any promises. I'll try.' If there was one thing she had learned in the past two weeks, it was not to underestimate him.

'All right, be stubborn. But keep that temper of yours under control at September Hill.'

'I'll do my best to be all sweetness and love,' Carey assured him. 'Just don't be fooled into thinking it's an invitation—it won't be.' But he was already on his way back to the office.

She shrugged and smiled. Perhaps for the first time in his life, Brandon Scott had run up against something he didn't quite know how to handle. It should be an enlivening experience for him, she decided, and yawned as she finished the apple. It would be a couple of hours till they would be landing at home, and she decided to go into the big bedroom and take a nap.

She had just curled up comfortably on the bed when the door opened, and Brandon came into the darkened cabin. She sat up straight, hair streaming about her shoulders. 'What are you doing here?' she gasped.

'Intending to do exactly what you are, I imagine,' he said coolly. 'Take a nap.' He yanked his necktie off and draped it across a chair next to the bed.

'In here? You can't. You promised.'

'Sorry, there is no alternative. I never realised that I'd need a two-bedroomed plane. Besides, it's a king-sized bed. You'll never know I'm here.' He sat down on the edge of the bed and took his shoes off.

Carey, offended, turned her back on him and curled up as close to the edge of the bed as possible, and soon her breathing was calm and even.

Brandon raised up on an elbow and reached out a gentle hand to stroke a lock of chestnut hair. Carey sighed in her sleep, and Brandon dropped the hair as if it had scorched him and turned over to seek sleep once more.

When Carey woke, it took her a moment to realise where she was. When she did, she was instantly indignant, for Brandon's body was curled around hers, his arm heavy across her, his hand casually cupping her breast while her hair was caught under his shoulder. 'I'll never know he's here—Ha!' she muttered furiously and struggled free. He murmured something, but he didn't wake, and she gathered up the hairpins that had worked themselves free as she slept, seized her hairbrush, and went out to the common room.

Brushing the tangles out of her hair helped, but she wouldn't feel back to normal until she had a fresh dress on, she thought. However, she wasn't crazy enough to venture back into the bedroom to hunt in her luggage. The last thing she wanted to do was rouse Brandon.

She was just pinning her hair up when there was a soft knock at the door. 'Come,' she called, still studying her reflection in the mirror, and went on when the door opened, 'Do you suppose there are some hairpins on board? I seem to have lost most of mine.'

A male voice answered, 'I wouldn't know. I'll ask the flight hostess.'

'I thought you were the flight hostess when you knocked.' She turned. 'David! I didn't expect you to be on duty.'

Lynne's fiancé looked taller and more handsome than ever in uniform, the gold stripes of a co-pilot on his sleeve. Carey wondered again, a little guiltily, if he wasn't just a shade too good-looking to be real.

'I came back to see that you're ready to land.'

'Already?'

The look David gave her was peculiar, as if he wondered how she could have lost three hours or so. 'Actually, we're a little behind schedule.'

Carey put in the last hairpin. 'I think that will stay up for a while,' she decided. 'Mr Scott is still asleep, if you wanted to talk to him.'

'Actually, Carey, it was you I wanted to talk to.'

She sat down in one of the deep chairs and indicated another, but David continued to stand, hands clasped easily behind his back.

'I don't quite know how you got Lynne off the hook this time,' he said, 'though I'm sure it helped to be engaged to the boss, but I want you to know I appreciate it. And she does, too, but I don't think she knows how to tell you. She takes you for granted.'

It was a pretty speech. Carey told herself that it wasn't fair to David to suspect him just because he was charming, but she never had really liked the man. 'I am her sister, after all. I do what I can.' She tried to shrug off the conversation. The enormity of what she had done for Lynne was too recent and painful to think about yet.

'Well, she appreciates it. We both do. I just wanted you to know, and I didn't have a chance to say so at your wedding.' He checked his watch. 'We're within half an hour of landing. You might want to wake Mr Scott.'

Carey did her best to look innocently exhausted. 'I just can't seem to get out of this chair,' she said. 'Perhaps you'd just tap on the cabin door?'

'I'd much rather not. Actually, I shouldn't be back here at all, but I wanted to make sure you know how Lynne feels.'

'It would be thoughtful of Lynne to learn to tell me how she feels,' Carey pointed out, 'but of course I appreciate the information no matter where it comes from.' She yawned. 'Please do knock on the cabin door as you go by, David. I just can't bring myself to stand up again.'

'I can't, Carey. The pilot who was supposed to make this run called in sick at the last minute, and instead of waiting for the standby to get there, the Captain called on me, since I'm next in line for a regular assignment anyway. It would be kind of embarrassing if Mr Scott found out I was even on board.'

'I see. I won't mention it to him.'

'You won't mention what, Carey?' Brandon asked.

David jumped and snapped a salute.

The man walks like a cat, Carey thought angrily. Nobody should have to put up with that. 'Brandon, you remember David Stratton, Lynne's fiancé,' she said.

'Mr Scott,' David said. 'I was just telling Carey how sorry I was that I had to leave your wedding reception early. I had to go out on a flight that evening.'

'I'm sorry you couldn't stay for all the fun. Will we be landing soon?'

'Yes, in just a few minutes. I'll be going back to the cockpit now, if you'll excuse me.' Another salute and he was gone.

'Handsome man.' Carey fastened her seat-belt and picked up the magazine she had abandoned earlier.

'I suppose I'll soon find out that you know every pilot on this airline by name.' He was still looking at the door, and there were two small furrows between his eyes.

'Not yet,' Carey said pleasantly. 'But I'm working on it.'

The Lincoln town car was waiting at the airport, and it whisked them through the city. They rode in silence, and Carey assumed that Brandon was already wondering what he would find at the main office. She then allowed herself to begin to think about the job she had taken on.

During their week's absence the leaves had reached their full glory. The oaks and maples were gorgeous, the leaves flaming against the golden brick mansion. Carey could see why fall at September Hill was Nancie's favourite season.

As the car pulled up in front of the house, Carey thought for an instant that she saw bars over the windows. Then she scolded herself for letting her imagination run away with her, and she walked quietly beside Brandon up the steps to the big front door.

The butler was at the door. 'Hello, Whitney,' Brandon said. It seemed strange to greet him by name, so Carey only smiled. As soon as she went inside, her heart sank, for there, lined up in the front hall, were all of the members of September Hill's staff, from housekeeper to lowliest maid. She had never seen so many uniforms in one place, she reflected.

Of course, her first encounter with the whole staff would have to be under Brandon's gaze, she thought, and became even more determined to put a good face on the situation.

She nodded to the housekeeper. 'It's good to be home, Mrs Whitney. Washington was beautiful, but not as inviting as September Hill, especially when the weather is so gorgeous.' If the angels in heaven take away one jewel from my heavenly crown each time I tell a lie, she thought, I'm in trouble already.

The housekeeper smiled proudly at the compliment and said, 'Mrs Scott, I'd like to present Grover, who will be your maid, if she is satisfactory.'

Carey looked into Grover's eyes, seeing warmth and friendly humour in the lines of the woman's face. It looked as if Nancie had again chosen well. Carey would need a friend at September Hill, especially one who had a sense of humour.

'We'll give it a try,' she said, and without waiting for an answer turned back to the housekeeper. 'Mrs Whitney, will you come up with me, please? I'd like to discuss a few things right away.' She started up the stairs and turned on the third step, knowing that the elevated position gave her an air of command.

'Thank you all for the welcome home,' she said, her eyes roaming over the faces below her. Three or four she recognised already. One, in particular, stood out—a young maid who seemed to have the giggles. Carey predicted that she would have trouble with that girl. 'I don't know all of your names yet, but I am going to learn. It's very nice to be home.' Another lie, she thought. As she turned to go on up the stairs she caught a glimpse of Brandon still standing in the doorway. He looked a little bemused, as though he hadn't recognised her. She smiled at him over the heads of the staff, a purely wicked smile. She had promised to run this house right, and she'd do it if it killed her. That was one place that the second Mrs Scott—whoever she would be— wouldn't easily erase Carey's influence.

As she climbed the stairs, Carey inspected, for the first time, the sculptures set into niches in the dark wood of the staircase. They were all by the same artist, she con- cluded, and wondered if the sculptor was one of Brandon's rare, interesting women.

In her own room, Carey sank on to the stool in front of her dressing table, kicking off her shoes with a sigh. 'Grover, if you would brush my hair? My brushes are in—oh, you already have them.'

'Of course, madam.' Grover unpinned the chestnut curls and began to massage her scalp.

Carey relaxed under the strong fingers for several minutes. Then she opened her eyes again to see Mrs Whitney standing near, trim in the tailored black uniform. 'I'd like to get acquainted with the staff as soon as possible,' Carey said, knowing that it was important she take charge, and let the staff know it, right away. If she didn't, she would never achieve control. 'I'd like for you to arrange for them to meet with me in groups, beginning tomorrow.'

'Certainly, madam.'

'Also, I'd like to know who prepares the menus.'

'The head cook does, with my approval.'

'I'd also like to see them every day.'

Mrs Whitney started to bristle a little, but Carey appeared not to notice. 'It's just a formality, of course,' she added. 'I can't imagine having to change anything; they're so well-planned to begin with.'

Mrs Whitney relaxed. 'Of course, madam.'

'Just one more thing—is there a small table that can be

set up in the alcove off the dining room? It's silly to use the big table for two people, and a little depressing, too.'

'I'll check, madam.' Mrs Whitney looked a little as if a cyclone was striking. 'There was something I needed to ask you also, madam. The small drawing room—it's full of wedding gifts. What would you like done with them?'

Send them back, Carey thought. The words actually trembled on her tongue. 'I'll look at them tomorrow. The whole room is full?'

Mrs Whitney nodded.

Of all the problems I didn't need, Carey thought. 'Thank you, Mrs Whitney.' After the woman had gone out of the room, Carey reached for a silver tray which held a stack of envelopes and message slips. 'Is this all of my mail?'

'I believe so, madam.'

Carey laughed at herself. 'I sounded as if I expected a bagful, didn't I? And by the way, please don't call me madam.' She studied the maid's sure hands in the mirror. 'I haven't had a maid before—you'll probably have to train me!'

The woman allowed a smile to cross her face. 'If you will pardon the impudence, Mrs Scott, I'd say you were born to the position.'

'That's encouraging.' Carey flipped through the mail again. 'I don't suppose you type?'

'Yes, I do. Mrs Dennis suggested that you might like me to double as a social secretary.'

'Mrs Dennis is a genius,' Carey said dryly. 'If you're going to be my secretary, I'd like to call you something else.'

'My given name is Anne.'

'That's much more comfortable, Anne.' Carey stood up to slip into the deep blue satin robe that the maid held out, then curled up into a brocade chair and started slitting envelopes open with the tiny silver knife.

Anne moved quietly about the room unpacking Carey's bags while she read her mail. Carey was only halfway through the stack when the telephone beside the bed rang, and Anne moved quickly to pick it up. 'Just a moment, I'll see if Mrs Scott is in,' she said and turned to Carey. 'It's a Miss Britton. She's called several times while you've been gone.'

Carey jumped up. 'I'm always in when Gail Britton calls,' she said firmly. 'She's my best friend.' She took the telephone. 'Hi, there. When are you coming to see me?'

'Carey! I nearly died when I got back last week and saw the story in *The Times*. I hardly knew if I should call—after all, I'm not accustomed to the likes of Mrs Brandon Scott.'

'It came up so suddenly, Gail. I wanted you to be my maid of honour, but Brandon was anxious to be married before he went to Washington, so I had to make do with Lynne.' It was the easiest way to explain the hurry. Carey thought that a lot of people were probably anticipating a Scott baby to arrive in about seven months. Nancie might even be among them—it would certainly explain why she had had no warning of her son's plans. But Carey didn't intend to let the gossips upset her. They would be proved wrong soon enough; it was relief enough to know that she wasn't pregnant. That really would have been the last straw, she thought.

'My heart is breaking. My best friend gets married in the wedding of the century, and I have to be out of town.'

'I'm bleeding for you, Gail. How is the child-care business?'

'Going very well. The Rocking Horse will be open for business the week after next, but the grand opening won't be for a month. Can you come and lend a little elegance?'

'Of course. Will you come out to the house tomorrow for lunch? I want you to see it.'

'And you also want to tell me all the details *The Times* didn't know about, I trust. But I can't come tomorrow; I have playground equipment being delivered. Would next week do?'

'Any day. Do you have a lot of kids signed up already?'

'About fifteen—that should be enough to start with. I'll probably have grey hair in a week as it is. There should be plenty of demand for the service. People are always looking for good babysitters, and they aren't ever going to stop having babies. Are you still planning on eight, by the way?'

'Not immediately,' Carey said dryly, and changed the subject before Gail could pursue it. 'And when the parents find out you're not only a good babysitter but a child psychologist, you'll have a waiting list so long some of the kids will grow up before they get in.'

'I could listen to that sort of encouragement all day, Carey, but here comes a prospective client. I'll see you later.'

Carey hung up the phone thoughtfully, wondering how much Gail already suspected. They had been best friends for years, and Gail wasn't a psychologist only by college degree. Carey sometimes wondered if her first words hadn't been 'And how does that make you feel?'

She shook open the letter she had just opened and wondered why she was getting mail from attorneys. And this one in particular, she wondered, after reading the letter. It was from a Mr Fellowes, and it asked the favour of a few minutes of her time to discuss personal business at the request of his valued client, Mr Brandon Scott.

What would Brandon's attorney have to discuss with her, Carey wondered. No use getting your hopes up, she told herself. Whatever it was, it certainly wasn't divorce, and there was little else an attorney could tell her that would be of interest right now.

CHAPTER SEVEN

'I DON'T believe it.' Carey stood in the centre of the small drawing room—which was called small only because it wasn't as large as the room next door— and stared at the piles of boxes that stood on the tables, balanced on the chairs, and threatened to eclipse the floor. She walked around the piles, stopping here and there to pick up a silver tray, to finger a silky monogrammed towel, to run a hand over the platinum rim on a wine goblet.

Mrs Whitney watched in silence for a moment, then handed her a book from a nearby table. 'Grover has been keeping a meticulous list as each gift is opened, with a complete description as well as the name of the giver. These things can go directly into service as soon as you have looked at them.'

'Which will be no small job,' Carey said absently as she picked up one of a set of silver napkin rings. 'There must be a hundred silver pieces here.'

'Probably. I can just start putting them away, if you like. There's no need for you to go through them all.'

'I want to, though. This is better than Christmas. And I can't write sensible thank-you letters if I haven't even looked at the gifts.'

Anne volunteered, 'I can do a lot of them, Mrs Scott. Some will have to get your personal attention, of course, but for most of them . . .'

'No. Everyone deserves a personal note.' She put the napkin ring down. 'You shouldn't have let me oversleep this morning, Anne,' she chided.

Anne just smiled. 'There's a china breakfast set here I think you'll like. It's a complete one. I thought perhaps you'd like to use it regularly.'

'Where is it?'

They were still hunting for the box when Whitney came in. 'Mrs Scott, Mrs Dennis is on the telephone. Can you come, or shall I take a message?'

Carey stood up, brushing off the packing chips that clung to her hands and sweater. 'I'll come. If you find that china, Anne, don't let it out of your sight!'

Nancie was exuberant. 'How was your trip, dear? Did you enjoy yourself?'

'Immensely,' Carey said, and resigned herself to an eternity in hell. Well, she told herself, maybe it wasn't really lying—she had enjoyed certain moments.

'Did you do much sight-seeing?'

'No. I just couldn't get excited by it with Brandon busy all of the time.' Not for anything would she hurt Nancie by telling her the whole truth about her honeymoon. Brandon might deserve that kind of treatment, but not Nancie.

'Some day we'll have to exchange travelogues over lunch,' Nancie said. 'Washington must have changed tremendously since I was there last. For the better, I hope. What I really called for was to ask if you and Brandon would like to have dinner with us tonight.'

'We'd love to—but I have a better idea. Why don't you two come here? Then you can help me decide what to do with the mess in the small drawing room!'

Nancie chuckled. 'They finally showed it to you, hmm? Well, I won't turn down the dinner invitation, but I have no intention of going through boxes. After all, it's my first evening with my son and his lovely wife, and I plan to enjoy it. I've certainly waited long enough for it.'

'But what do I do with all of the gifts?' Carey wailed.

'It's simple, dear. First you have a couple of the maids take everything out of the boxes and get rid of all the packing. Then you ask your new treasure, Anne Grover, to sort it all into piles— separating the tasteful from the gaudy. Then you work through this afternoon, sending the gaudy stuff to the attic, turning the silver over to Whitney with a grand gesture, and graciously allowing Mrs Whitney to disperse the rest. What is so difficult about that?'

Carey was laughing. 'And that's it? I can take care of the whole roomful in an hour?'

'That's what household help is for, Carey. Every woman should have it. Just learn to delegate, dear.'

'Delegate I shall, Nancie. Will you still come to dinner?'

'We'll be honoured. By the way, there are some stationery samples in the small desk in the morning room. I didn't know what you liked, so I had several made up. And now I'm positively going to stop interfering in your business any more!'

Carey gave the recommended instructions in the drawing room and went on to her morning room with a lighter heart. She sorted through stationery samples and debated between a cream-coloured heavy bond with block letters that said simply 'September Hill' and a version in pastels with her initials in darker shades.

Then it occurred to her that she should check with Brandon about his schedule for the evening. It would be just her luck if, since she had invited guests, he had already made other plans. With one of his interesting women, perhaps.

As she waited for her phone call to be transferred through the layers of authority, she could almost see it rising from floor to floor of the office building. She tapped a pencil on the desk blotter while she waited, wondering if he had a private line directly to his office. He must have one, she decided; she couldn't imagine Michelle Lantry or any of the other proud beauties he had dated waiting long minutes for calls to be transferred. And if he did have such a phone, she wondered if he would ever give her the number or if she would always have to go through this mess every time she wanted to talk to him.

'What is it, Carey?' His voice was brusque.

'I've invited Nancie and Clarke to dinner tonight. I hope you hadn't made other plans.'

'I hadn't. Is that all you called about?'

'Yes. I'm sorry. It's obvious I shouldn't have bothered.' Carey was irate, as angry at herself as at him. Whatever had made her think that he would approve of anything she did? Of course, if she hadn't consulted him, he would have been angry about that too.

'That is what I have an appointments secretary for. Why don't you talk to her about it?' The line clicked off.

'Gee, thanks,' Carey muttered, and was still simmering a few moments later when a deep throaty voice said, 'This is Lisa, Mr Scott's appointments secretary. Can I help you?'

Carey's eyebrows raised. With that voice, I'll bet her phone number is in the wallet of every obscene caller in the metropolitan area, she thought. Her voice is certainly interesting. I wonder if the rest of her lives up to it.

'I've been told I'm to talk to you whenever I need to get something on Mr Scott's calendar,' she said. Her voice showed her irritation.

'That would be best,' the girl agreed. 'I don't mean to be impudent, Mrs Scott, but you shouldn't be upset. Heads are rolling all over the building today. There are days like that around here, you know. If you call me first, then I can fit your message in when it will be the least interruption.'

Carey could see the sense in that, though she still had difficulty in accepting the olive branch. She had worked there long enough herself to see heads roll. But if she had been an ordinary wife, she told herself, she would not allow any secretary to tell her when she could talk to her husband. And she wouldn't allow the husband to foist her off on a secretary either.

She put the phone down hard and turned back to the notepaper, deciding to order both of the samples. After all, if she was going to have to put up with that kind of treatment, she might as well have some of the perks of wealth to make up for it a little. In fact, she decided rebelliously, trousseau or no trousseau, she was in the mood for a shopping spree.

What she wasn't in the mood for was Lynne, but she

had little choice a few minutes later when Whitney tapped on the door of the morning room to tell her that Miss Forsythe and Mr Stratton had called. Almost before he could finish his sentence, Lynne slipped past him and came in. She leaned over the desk and put a casual kiss on Carey's cheek, then said, 'I love this room.' She tossed herself down on to the couch and added, 'Bring me something cold, Whitney.'

Whitney's face was implacable. He appeared not to have heard Lynne, as he looked to Carey for further instructions. 'Iced tea would be fine, Whitney,' she said gently. 'Thank you.' The butler disappeared, the ramrod stiffness of his spine showing what he thought of the way the young miss was trying to run this house.

'Be sure there's plenty of lemon,' Lynne called after him.

David came in. 'Hi, Carey. I hope you don't mind; I stopped to look at one of the paintings in the next room. A Degas, isn't it?'

Carey nodded. 'May I ask what brings you both here on a fine morning?'

Lynne sat up. 'Oh, we were just driving by and decided to say welcome home. I thought you'd be headfirst into all those boxes. You certainly got a lot of wedding gifts.'

No doubt Lynne had seen every one of them. Before Carey could say what she was thinking, Whitney returned with a silver tray on which rested three picture-perfect glasses of iced tea. He served them silently and merely nodded when Carey told him, 'Thank you.'

Lynne sniffed. 'You'll never get any respect from the servants as long as you treat them like that, Carey. You have to show them who's boss.'

David interrupted. 'Lynne, it's Carey's house. Let her run it the way she wants.' He sipped his iced tea.

Thanks, David, that's gracious of you, Carey thought. 'How was the fishing?' she asked.

'Oh, it was all right. I didn't do much fishing actually. The peace and quiet are what I really go for.'

Lynne pouted. 'You only go to get away from me.'

'That isn't true, Lynne.'

'Prove it to me. Stay home this week.'

'I can't. I promised Pete I'd go.' He patted Lynne on the head as if she were a puppy and smiled down at her. Lynne sighed and smiled and laid her head on his shoulder. Apparently he was forgiven.

If there ever was a pair that deserve each other! Carey thought.

'Expensive taste in art your husband's got,' David commented, looking at the landscape that hung on the morning room wall. 'He must have a couple of million tied up on the walls around here—not to mention the sculpture.'

Carey tried to conceal her discomfort at the idea of discussing Brandon's collection. 'I hadn't added it up.'

He winked at her. 'You'd better start. It never hurts to know what he's worth, you know.' He stood up and pulled Lynne to her feet. 'We'd better go if I'm driving up to the cabin this afternoon. Thanks for the tea.'

Lynne turned at the door. 'I'll come out some day while David's communing with nature and we'll have lunch and go shopping. How about it, Carey?'

'I'll call you,' Carey said faintly. When they had gone she sank into a chair. She put a hand to her aching head and asked herself why she had got herself into this mess for that ungrateful little brat. 'If I had told her just why I was sitting here,' Carey muttered, 'she'd have taken it as a compliment.' She sat still for a long time, and then went to get an aspirin.

Carey was dressing in her room when Brandon came home that evening, so she didn't see him until they met in the drawing room a few minutes before Clarke and Nancie were due to arrive. She was still angry about the way he had treated her on the phone that morning and she was determined to let him know about it.

Brandon was already in the room when Carey came in, and he glanced at his watch as she entered. She was outraged afresh. Perhaps some day he would learn that punctuality was as important to her as it seemed to be to him.

A tray of glasses and a decanter of sherry stood at his elbow. The decanter was full, and no used glass was in sight. She wondered if that was for her benefit, since she hadn't hesitated to tell him what she thought of his drinking habits.

'Would you like some sherry?' he asked.

'Please,' she said coolly. She watched as he poured the wine, took the glass, and sipped.

'What's bothering you?' he asked.

'Do you really need to be told?'

He set his glass down with a crash. 'I hope you give a better performance when our guests come in.'

'Oh, I will. I hope you will, too,' Carey said sweetly. 'Right now you look like a spoiled little boy.'

'What is the matter with you? Could you just thaw out a little?'

'Me thaw out? What's the matter with you, that you couldn't take two minutes to talk to me on the phone? I'll bet Michelle didn't have to make appointments with your secretary.'

'Is that's what's wrong with you?' His face cleared. 'All right, I was hard on you today. While I was gone everything seems to have fallen apart, and you called right in the middle of it all. And Michelle had to wait sometimes too, in case you're jealous.'

'Don't flatter yourself, Brandon. I didn't interrupt you on purpose, and I think you could have been civil to me.'

'If you want me to be civil, you might try it yourself. It would make a nice change.'

Before she could retort, their guests came in. Nancie fluttered across the room to hug Carey. 'Darling, you're radiant. It must have been Washington, right, Brandon?'

To Carey's surprise, Brandon's laugh was easy and natural. 'Of course it was the trip,' he agreed. 'I can't think of anything else it might have been. Mother, you look splendid. Clarke—' he extended a hand '— I'm anxious to get you back to the office.'

'Not as anxious as I am to get back,' Clarke laughed.

'Young Mason is good but he needs a few more years on him before he will be ready to take over. And with Carey's gift for public relations gone, it's been a little difficult at Universal. I'm thinking I chose the wrong time to be married.' He looked at Carey with a loving smile, but she was achingly aware of the bite of sarcasm under the compliment, as he brushed a light kiss on to her cheek.

'No business, gentlemen,' Nancie announced, her eyes gleaming at the display of affection. 'Those are doctor's orders, as well as mine, Brandon. How did I do at choosing you a maid, Carey?'

'Anne's a gem, and she's even offered to take over my correspondence. I'm beginning to think I couldn't live without her.' Carey pulled casually away from Brandon, picked up her wine glass, and drew Nancie a little away from the men. She sat down in a comfortable chair.

'Of course you could do without her. It will just be a lot more convenient with her around.'

Brandon had followed them. He sat down on the arm of Carey's chair, his hand resting on the nape of her neck, and asked lazily, 'How much did you tell this gem I'd pay her, Mother?'

Nancie laughed. 'You'll find out when the next payroll comes through. I don't want to ruin your digestion tonight.' She turned immediately to Carey. 'I thought that colour was a good choice when you selected it.'

'When you chose it, you mean,' Carey interposed. She was doing her best to sit absolutely still and not react to the light pressure of Brandon's hand on the back of her neck.

'But it looks even better on you than I expected,' Nancie said. 'I'm beginning to think you should always wear yellow. Would you get me a glass of sherry, dear?' she asked Brandon. As he moved away, she added, 'You know who Michelle Lantry is, don't you, Carey?'

'Of course. We met her in Washington.'

'Brandon's known her a lot longer than that.'

'And a lot better, too,' Carey murmured. 'The rumour-mill had them engaged, didn't it?'

'I'm glad it didn't take you by surprise. I was afraid it would come as an unpleasant shock. She called me today—she must have just got back into town—and I venture to guess that means trouble.'

'Oh, Michelle doesn't bother me.' None of Brandon's old girl-friends do, she thought.

'Did I hear you say something about Michelle?' Brandon handed Nancie her glass.

'I was just telling your mother how very interesting Michelle was in Washington,' Carey said sweetly. Brandon frowned.

They had dinner by candlelight on the terrace, which faced west to the setting sun and the air was unseasonably warm. The tapers and the flowers in the centrepiece were the same jonquil yellow as Carey's dress. Nancie smoothed her own turquoise chiffon and said, 'Frankly, I'm jealous because I never thought of matching the decorations to my clothes. And if you smile and tell me it was a coincidence, I won't believe you.'

Carey smiled. 'It was just a coincidence, Nancie.'

'Ha!'

'I didn't want to give up what may be our last warm evening,' Carey continued.

'It's beautiful out here, isn't it?' Nancie gestured towards the wide lawn. 'You just got back in time for the leaves. By the weekend, they'll be falling.'

'They wouldn't dare.'

'Unfortunately, they don't belong to Scott Enterprises, so Brandon can't tell them what to do. Which reminds me, we neglected to buy you a winter coat. Would you like mink?'

'I would not. I couldn't bear to think of the poor little animals. I'll stick to something that the animal doesn't have to die to produce—like wool.'

'You'll freeze.'

'Nancie, I've lived in this climate for years with a good Republican cloth coat, and I'm still fairly warm-blooded.'

'You just come along with me when I buy mine, and you'll change your mind,' Nancie predicted.

Despite Nancie's prohibition, the two men talked business throughout dinner. After the table was cleared, Brandon reached for Carey's hand and held it firmly, absently rubbing her knuckles against his chin. At least, Carey was certain that the gesture looked like an absent-minded loving caress, but she was equally certain that it had been carefully planned. Nancie was watching the byplay fondly, she noticed. Carey tried to pull away, but Brandon's grip tightened, the wedding band on his finger cutting into her hand.

When they rose from the table, Nancie murmured to Carey, 'Won't you try to take Clarke's mind off the office, dear? I'm going to drag Brandon out to the garden for a while, before he gets so involved with you that he forgets we're here.'

'I'll do my best.' Carey would have walked through hot coals right then to be rid of Brandon. 'Whitney, we'll have coffee and dessert in the library a little later, please.'

'Brandon, take me for a walk,' Nancie demanded. 'I want to see the garden one last time before winter sets in.' She slipped a hand through his arm. 'I wonder what it will be like next year.'

'It will feature Carey's favourite flowers. The gardener has already fallen in love with her—he brought her a bouquet this morning.' Their voices faded as they strolled off.

'If we're not having dessert right away, perhaps you'll allow me to sit here and have a cigar,' Clarke said, indicating a nearby chair.

'Of course, Clarke.' Carey perched on the terrace rail.

He lit the cigar and said, 'I'm delighted that you and Nancie are getting along so well. Of course, I hardly expected it to turn out this way. How you must have laughed at me when I assumed that day you visited me at the hospital that you hated Brandon.' His eyes, suddenly shrewd, rested on her, and Carey squirmed a little. She didn't want to lie to Clarke. But after a moment, he looked at the glowing tip of his cigar and began to speak gently of other things.

Out in the garden, the air was warm as mother and son strolled through the formal gardens. The last fall blossoms were fading and many of the beds were ready for winter. Tonight was unseasonably warm, probably the last day of an Indian summer.

'How is she doing, Brandon?' Nancie prompted. 'You weren't joking about the garden being planted with her favourites, were you?'

'No. The gardener would never listen to your suggestions, would he?'

'Never. He'd act as if he agreed with me and then he'd do as he liked. I think I'm jealous,' Nancie mused.

'And she's set Whitney's hair on end two nights in a row.'

'Dinner on the terrace, and what else?'

'Last night she made him set up a small table in the dining room alcove. He looked very disapproving, but it didn't bother her a bit.'

Nancie chuckled. 'Good, she's taking control. I can just see Whitney's face.'

Brandon strolled on in silence. 'Would you like to tell me why you hired Anne Grover, Mother?' he asked finally.

It didn't bother Nancie. 'So the security check caught her. I assumed it would.'

'You don't pass off a former policewoman as an ordinary lady's maid for very long, Mother. You forget that the man running my security operation used to work for the FBI.'

'I didn't forget it for a moment. I just thought that a little extra protection wouldn't be a bad idea, especially since Carey has never had to learn the sort of caution she'll need now.' She stooped to inspect a shrub. 'Does Carey know it?'

'No, and I don't plan to tell her. Just as I won't tell her why I insisted she sell her car, even if she does think I'm an insufferable dictator for making her do it.

'I'm glad you did. You could never convince her that there are people out there who wouldn't hesitate to kidnap or kill her. At least when she has the limousine, she won't ever be alone. Have there been any threats?'

'Just the usual crackpots. Nothing serious yet.'

'Well, I trust Anne Grover. She will be so subtle about teaching our young lady to look out for herself that Carey will never know she's been taught.' Then she chuckled. 'I wish I could have seen Whitney's face. That is a girl after my own heart, Brandon. The minute I got to know her, I knew where she belonged. I'm so glad you found her.'

Brandon was silent a moment, then he said, 'I know, Mother. I'm a very lucky man.' His mouth twisted a little as he said it, but Nancie didn't see.

Brandon's attorney, Mr Fellowes, was on time to the moment. Carey invited him into her morning room, which was sunny and bright. She tucked away the stack of thank-you notes she had been writing and sat down in a pale gold chair. Mr Fellows chose the matching couch, and put his briefcase on the coffee table, lining it up neatly parallel to the table's edge.

'I won't take much of your time, Mrs Scott,' he said quickly. 'I know you're wondering why I wanted to talk to you. Mr Scott asked me to tell you about the financial provisions he has made for you, both now and in the event of his untimely death.' The little lawyer nearly crossed himself at the thought.

'Surely it isn't necessary to go into all of the details.'

'Mr Scott was quite definite about wanting you to know all of the arrangements.' He unsnapped the locks on the briefcase. 'I've prepared a summary for your files. Mr Scott has established a small trust fund in your name;

the dividends will be paid directly to your bank. This will be spending money only—your clothing and personal expenditures are to be billed directly to him. I have approximate amounts on this summary. These are quarterly figures, you know.'

Carey, who hadn't known, was intrigued. She glanced down the column of figures, drawing her own conclusions. She had not expected Brandon to be generous in the matter of money, other than for her adornment as the piece of art he apparently thought her to be. Once again he had surprised her.

'You'll want to talk to his accountant, who can give you more details,' Mr Fellowes advised. 'This will be an income for your lifetime, of course. If you should die, the principal reverts to Mr Scott or to his estate. Now in the event of his death . . . '

Carey nodded her understanding. It didn't surprise her that Brandon was adding a financial incentive for her to continue in the marriage. Her mind wandered as Mr Fellowes droned on about trust funds, housing expenses, upkeep on September Hill, charitable donations . . .

Then her attention snapped back to the attorney as he said, 'All of this, of course, presumes that Mr Scott is survived by at least one legal direct descendant. Whether that child is male or female would make no difference. The Scott Foundation, the division he has set up to handle his charitable donations, will be expanded to protect the assets of the corporation. Here is the way that arrangement will work.' He handed her another sheet of paper.

Carey took the document in a suddenly nerveless hand. So Brandon's campaign had started in earnest.

'Of course the foundation would assume all expenses relating to September Hill. Mr Scott would naturally want the children raised here.'

So now he was talking of more than one. 'Naturally,' Carey said. Her voice was icy.

'In the event of Mr Scott's death without surviving

children, the estate would still be transferred into the control of the foundation, but it would be operated for the sole bemefit of Mr Scott's selected charities. Your trust fund would be unaffected, but September Hill would become the foundation's home, and you would receive no additional income.'

'Of course not,' Carey murmured. 'And if there is a divorce?' Mr Fellowes raised his eyebrows, and Carey shrugged her shoulders. 'I'm certain Mr Scott wanted you to cover every possibility,' she said sweetly.

'If there were no children, then the principal of your trust fund would revert to him.'

'In other words, I wouldn't get a dime.'

He looked shocked. 'To put it bluntly—no, Mrs Scott.'

'Thank you for your frankness, Mr Fellowes.' So Brandon wasn't being so generous after all. In fact, he was blackmailing again. He wanted a child, and if she gave him one, he would be generous. At least until he decided he wanted to be free of her. If she didn't give him a child . . . No wonder he was so certain that she would change her mind.

Hell, Carey told herself, the income from the trust fund would be adequate for anything she needed. Probably she could save most of it, and she wasn't afraid to work. She would just have to be careful not to let this life of ease make her forget that some day she would have to take care of herself again.

If he thinks this little trick will get him anything, he's going to find out what stubborn means, she vowed. He probably thinks I'll hand him an engraved invitation tonight!

She looked up to find the attorney's questioning eyes fixed on her. 'Go on,' she said. 'I'm sure there is more.'

'There is one more provision you should be aware of.'

'Why am I not surprised?' Carey mused. Inside, she was screaming.

'You will have joint guardianship—along with the trustees of the foundation—of the children. If you should remarry after Mr Scott's death, and the trustees feel that this is not to the advantage of the children, they can seek to have your guardianship terminated. That's for the benefit of the children, you see—don't you?'

'After all, no one would expect me to have their best interests at heart,' Carey snapped and caught herself up short. Why get upset about something that would never happen?

Knowing Brandon as she did, she suspected there was already a list of potential husbands to whom the trustees were ordered to object. He intended to keep control of her whether he lived or died, she fumed. Then she put the brakes on her anger. He couldn't take children away from her if the children didn't exist.

'Mrs Scott, I'm sorry if you've been hurt by this,' Mr Fellowes said. 'Your husband has your best interests at heart; he feels you should know . . .'

'Is that all?' Carey interrupted.

'Yes, except for a few forms for you to sign. Your permission to set up bank accounts . . .'

Carey signed it silently.

'And this one merely states . . .' He took a deep breath and plunged. 'That you received all of the information pertaining to Mr Scott's will and that you agree to the conditions . . .'

Was there anything the man didn't think of? Carey raged, but she didn't say a word. Her hand shook on the pen as she signed the document. It was all she could do to smile as she stood up, ending the interview. It isn't Mr Fellowes' fault, she told herself. He is just the bearer of the bad news. But it would have been satisfying to have thrown something at him; no doubt that was why Brandon hadn't told her about all this himself.

The house seemed stifling, so she walked out through the garden. The chrysanthemums in the centre of the circular drive were the last of the season, and she leaned over to sniff one. 'What will I do when these are gone?' she asked the gardener, who was trimming off the blooms which had passed their prime.

'I guess you'll have to settle for the greenhouse,' the leathery man said. He saw her hand hovering near a stem and his face crinkled into a smile. 'Go ahead and pick one,' he said. 'After all, they're yours, aren't they?'

Carey laughed and plucked a perfect flower, tucking it into the belt loop on her white slacks. The shaggy salmon-pink flower made the perfect foil for the royal blue of her blouse. 'Sometimes I think you must raise these in the greenhouse and then move them out here when I'm not looking,' she accused.

'You wouldn't expect me to tell you if I did, would you?' the gardener asked.

'No.' Carey sat down on the stone kerbing and said, 'What are you going to plant today?'

'I'm going to repot orchids.'

'What about poinsettias for Christmas? Will we have some?'

'A hundred if you want. There hasn't been much Christmas decorating here the last few years, since Mrs Dennis has her own home, and the boss doesn't much care.'

'Well, I care. I'll take every poinsettia you can come up with. I've never had flowers like this before, and I love it. And thank you for the marigolds in my morning room—they're beautiful.'

'Marigolds?' The gardener's voice was innocent.

'You aren't fooling anyone. Flowers every morning— and you've been seen delivering them.' She turned her attention back to the flowerbed. 'I want poppies next spring. Acres and acres of them, just like in Oz.'

'I don't think the boss would like it if we tore up the lawn.'

'No, I don't suppose he would, the spoil-sport. Can I have at least one bed of poppies?' If I'm still here, Carey thought. If I haven't lost my head completely and committed murder so that I'm sitting in a prison cell next spring.

The big Lincoln pulled noiselessly up to the front door, and Carey jumped up and ran to meet Gail.

Gail looked the same as always, slim and small, with her red hair cut short and every strand in place. Carey had never thought of Gail as the type to romp with a child. In fact, Carey could never imagine Gail with a child even on her lap. But the girl spoke the language of small children; whenever they were in her presence, tots went straight to her. That was bad enough, Carey thought, but the truly aggravating thing was that Gail could emerge from a romp with a dozen children and still look as if she belonged in a display window, and she told Gail that.

The redhead merely laughed and gave her a hug. 'If you're right, it should come in handy at the Rocking Horse. It will give the clients confidence in my ability.' She looked around the front hall, studying the waxed parquet floor, the hanging staircase, the sculpture. 'When you move up in the world, you do it with a vengeance, my dear!' Her eyes were troubled, though, as she studied Carey's face.

Carey tried to laugh it off, and it wasn't until after lunch, when they had retreated to comfort and privacy in Carey's upstairs sitting room, that Gail finally said, 'Come on. Spill it. Something is terribly wrong here.'

So Carey told her about Lynne, the stolen necklace, Brandon's threats, everything right through to the discussion with Mr Fellowes that morning.

Gail was silent for a long time. 'Your little sister really landed you in a tub of hot water this time,' she said finally. 'When are you going to stop trying to paddle her canoe as well as your own?'

'She's my sister. I have to do what I can for her.'

'Shouldn't she be doing what she could for herself?' Gail asked tartly. 'All right, I don't want to quarrel with you about Lynne. Do you know what I'd do?'

'What?'

'Leave him. Just walk out. He can't file charges against Lynne now without looking ridiculous, and Brandon Scott doesn't sound like the type who would risk that.'

Carey shook her head. 'I can't. You have no idea of the power that man has.'

'I suppose you're right,' Gail agreed reluctantly. 'And I imagine it would be a little difficult to find another job with an airline after this fiasco.' She shrugged. 'So you're determined to make the best of it?'

'I have to be. It isn't just me, but Lynne's job as well. He might not file charges against her, but he could blacklist her.' She curled up tighter in her chair. 'It can't last long, anyway. He's getting tired of it already.'

'I hope you're right, of course. In the meantime, don't you adore this house?'

'Oh, yes. I'm having my first cocktail party this evening. Nancie's going to hold my hand through it. Why don't you stay and meet her? Getting to know her was almost worth the whole thing.'

'I can't. The city inspector is coming this afternoon— it's the last formality before getting my licence. I'll be honest about it; some of your new friends could do me a lot of good. In fact, if you could just announce discreetly that of course your children will be attending the Rocking Horse . . .'

Carey threw a pillow at her. At least I don't have that complication, thank God.'

'I'm sorry. I shouldn't have teased about it. By the way, I brought the clipping from *The Times*, if you want it. I thought you might like an extra for your scrapbook.'

'I haven't even seen it.'

'How could you miss it?' Gail pulled the clipping from her purse.

It was a full-page spread with several pictures, including a colour shot of them dancing the last waltz alone on the floor. The young photographer must have made a good sale.

'We put a good face on it, didn't we?' Carey mused.

'Cameras don't lie. I'd have sworn you were in love. If I were you, Carey, I'd get in touch with that photographer. He's got talent, and I think you should let him photograph you formally.'

'Who wants a picture of me? I can see myself in the mirror. Let's go look at all my gifts—you'll love it!'

'When is Lynne getting married?' Gail asked as they browsed through the presents in the small drawing room. Carey had followed Nancie's advice up to a point, but had left the display, thinking that Brandon might like to see it. Since he had shown no interest, she planned to ask the staff to put everything away that afternoon.

'They haven't set a date yet—David seems to keep finding reasons to delay it. Lynne calls me at least once a day. She got very upset with me when she discovered she was banned from Brandon's plane.'

'Doesn't she know what happened?' Gail was astounded.

'No. I didn't think there was any point in telling her.'

'So you just meekly gave up your freedom and didn't bother to tell her what you had done to get her off the hook?'

'I didn't want her to know, Gail. Lynne would never had missed an opportunity to remind me of it.'

'Sometimes you amaze me, Carey. Aren't you ever going to tell her no?'

'I have. I refused to ask Brandon to put her back on the plane.'

Gail shook her head. Then she glanced at her watch. 'I have to go, Carey. Will you be able to come to the open house?'

'Of course. I'll be glad to provide as much elegance and publicity as I can for the occasion, even if I don't plan to reserve places for any offspring of mine.'

'I'll keep a spot open in each class, just in case,' Gail teased. 'Who knows? Brandon's next offer may be one you can't refuse!'

CHAPTER EIGHT

'WHAT if nobody comes?' Carey moved an ashtray half an inch to the left.

'They'll come.' Nancie didn't look up from her magazine. 'Don't be so frightened. It's only a cocktail party.'

'I wonder if Michelle will show up.'

'Don't borrow trouble. She'll turn up soon enough, no doubt. I don't mind telling you, Carey, I prayed Brandon wouldn't marry that girl.'

'I thought they got along very well.'

Nancie's eyes were sharp, but before she could say anything, Brandon came in. He came across the room and put his arm around Carey. 'Sorry to be late, darling,' he said.

She spread her hands across his chest to prevent him from pulling her too close. Brandon smiled and tipped her face up, his hand sliding sensuously along her throat and then moving to cup the back of her head.

'Don't muss my hair,' she begged.

'If anyone does, it will be you,' he said softly. 'Hold still.' He put a warm kiss on her lips which Carey suffered in silence. She was finally ready to admit that Brandon was a better actor than she was.

'Did you have a long day?' It was a safe question; he was usually gone when she got up. She planned it that way so she could breakfast in her sitting room without worrying about her meal being spoiled by his presence. In fact, this was the first time she had seen him all day.

'It wasn't too bad—last week's mess is finally straightening itself out. I think our first guests are arriving. Mother, are you greeting them with us?'

'Oh, no. I'm only here for moral support.'

Carey needed that reassurance, for among the early arrivals was Mrs Harrison Ayres. Tonight she was

110

wearing diamonds, stones so big that they looked as if they must have come from a dime store.

When they had been introduced at the wedding reception, Carey had been so preoccupied that she hadn't paid much attention to the woman. Today the sparkling eyes seemed to slice through her and announce, 'I know why you're standing there! And I could tell, if I liked.'

It was silly to be thinking that, Carey told herself. The most that Millicent Ayres could know—or think she knew—was that Lynne was a thief. She couldn't possibly know any more.

After Mrs Ayres moved on, Nancie came by to whisper, 'Don't fret so. After you meet Millicent a few times you'll learn to ignore those mismatched refugees from the jewellery stores that she wears. You won't even see them any more.'

'I was just wondering. Is there a Mr Harrison Ayres?' Carey whispered back. 'And does she call him Harry?'

'I presume he exists. But nobody's ever seen him.' Nancie moved on.

Carey wondered what explanation Brandon had given Millicent for ignoring the matter of her missing necklace. Funny that she hadn't considered that before. But she soon forgot the woman, for the drawing room was pleasantly full and conversation buzzed around them.

When the arrivals slowed, Brandon reached for two glasses from a nearby waiter's tray and handed one to Carey. 'Let's circulate,' he suggested, and linked his arm with hers, smiling down at her.

It was a heart-stopping smile. Carey thought, if I didn't know him so well, I might be taken in by it.

Whitney came through the crowd and stopped them. 'Mrs Scott, Miss Britton is on the phone. She said it was important that she talk to you.'

'I'll take it up in my room. Brandon, if you will excuse me?' Gail had left just a couple of hours earlier. If she was calling now it must be important.

Carey stopped at the top of the stairs and kicked her shoes off. It was a relief at least to be rid of those for a few moments. She felt she deserved a break.

She crossed the deeply carpeted sitting room silent-footed. A movement from the bedroom caught her eye, and she moved towards the door to see what it was. She was just in time to see the upstairs maid, at the mirrored dressing table, slip one of the monogrammed silver and crystal perfume bottles into the pocket of her uniform.

'Good evening,' Carey said pleasantly.

The maid's nervous leap would have been enough to convict her without the evidence of what Carey had seen. Carey moved into the bedroom, considering what she should do. The maid was one she had had trouble with before, and Carey had wondered if it was her imagination or if things—tiny things—were really missing from her room.

'I'm going to go answer a telephone call,' she said firmly. 'By the time I finish, I shall expect that bottle to be back on the dressing table and you to be gone. You will find Mrs Whitney in the kitchen if you'd care to resign. If you don't care to, you will have written notice in the morning. I trust I've made myself clear?'

Hatred snapped in the maid's eyes, but there was fear in them too. She said, 'Yes, madam,' in the least servile tone Carey had ever heard. But she was fumbling in her pocket as Carey turned away.

Anne Grover came in as Carey reached for the telephone. 'I saw you coming upstairs,' she said. 'Is there something you need help with?'

'Yes. Please see that the little maid who's presently in my bedroom goes out the back door as soon as possible. Don't leave her alone—I just fired her.'

The expression on Anne's face almost frightened Carey. 'I wish you hadn't done that, Mrs Scott.'

'Why on earth not? She a thief!'

'Yes, madam. But it would have been safer not to have done it yourself.'

'Safer? Are you saying . . . Oh, Anne, for heaven's sake!' Carey picked up the phone. 'Gail, what is it?'

There was a muffled sob on the other end of the line.

'It's the Rocking Horse, Carey. I can't get my licence. The zoning change for the building didn't go through. I can't open—not next week, not ever.'

'Oh, Gail! What happened?'

'I don't know. It was all arranged—just this last formality. They said some of the neighbours were concerned about so many children being there. But there's a fenced-in play area. It's not as if they'll be roaming the streets.'

'What are you going to do?'

'I don't know, Carey. I've already exhausted all of the protests. I suppose I'll salvage what I can from the building and look for a new location. I shouldn't even have started till the paperwork was all done, but they assured me there would be no problem.'

'Gail, I'm so sorry.'

'It helped, just to tell you about it. I've kept you from your party too long now. Thanks, Carey.'

'I wish there was something I could do.' After she put the phone down, Carey sat there for a few minutes, seeing her friend's dream go up in flames. And there was little she could do to help. If Gail needed further financing, perhaps Carey's new trust fund would allow her to assist. But there were more problems than mere money could solve. Then she shook herself, put her shoes back on, and returned to her party.

As she came up behind Brandon, she heard him say quietly, 'Millicent, if I hear of you making any more remarks about my wife, you will never be invited here again.' Mrs Ayres had no reply, but she shot a stabbing look at Carey as Brandon turned to greet her.

Carey shivered, and Brandon drew her hand through his arm and said, 'Don't let the old witch bother you, Carey. She just needs to be threatened now and then to keep her straight.'

'What was she saying about me?'

'Don't worry about it. People only believe about half of what she says anyway.'

'Oh, really?' Carey's tone was dry.

Brandon had the grace to flush. 'What was your call about?'

Carey forgot Millicent Ayres. 'I've told you about Gail, haven't I, Brandon? The child psychologist who's opening a new day-care centre?'

'I think so.'

'At the last minute the zoning change for her building fell through. She's got every cent she has tied up in the building and equipment, and now she can't get her licence. She was ready to open next week.'

Just then a quartet of guests swooped down on them and there was no chance to say anything else. As Carey circulated about the room, her mind was torn. Would it help Gail if she were to plead with Brandon to do what he could for her? Or was Gail's problem too small for him to bother with? He probably wouldn't want to be bothered, she decided. After all, day-care centres were small potatoes. And what had he meant, she wondered, by saying that people only believed half of what Millicent Ayres said? He had certainly believed the story of the disappearing necklace.

It seemed hours before the last of the guests left and Whitney closed the front door for the final time. Even Nancie had gone. Carey turned towards the library. 'I'm going to put my feet up,' she told Brandon.

He followed her into the room. 'You did a beautiful job tonight, Carey. For a first party, it was superb.'

'Thank you.' Carey tossed herself down into a chair and reached for the catch on her sandal.

'Let me.' He dropped to one knee beside her chair, and gently removed her shoes. 'Why you women wear these things is beyond me. Does that feel better?'

'Much better. But if you're hoping to capitalise on the suggestions Mr Fellowes planted this morning, you can forget it.'

Brandon rocked back on his heels. 'So he was out here?'

'Yes, and he carried out your instructions to the letter. Aren't you getting in a hurry? For all you know I'm already pregnant and all of that effort was wasted.'

'You're not. You've been cocky the last few days. If you thought you might be pregnant, you'd have been very upset.'

'That's the understatement of the year. At any rate, my answer is still no. No amount of money would make it worth my while to sleep with you.'

Brandon stared up at her impassively. 'That's one good thing about you, Carey,' he observed. 'A man always knows exactly where he stands.'

She leaned forward, her anger forgotten. 'Let me go, Brandon,' she pleaded. 'Can't you see what this is doing to both of us? Please, let me go.'

He shook his head.

There was a commotion outside the door, and suddenly it was flung open. Michelle Lantry stood on the threshold in a dress that revealed as much as it covered, a dress only a model could have carried off. She was saying over her shoulder, 'Whitney, Mr Scott is always at home for me; aren't you, darling?' She turned towards them and her laugh trilled as she saw Brandon kneeling at Carey's feet. 'Dancing attendance on the little *Hausfrau*, Bran? How charming of you—and how tedious. But I'm sure she's flattered by the attention. I'm sorry to be so late for your party, Carey, but since my invitation included dinner, I thought perhaps I'd be forgiven.'

Brandon had risen to his feet, and Michelle fluttered over to him. 'How am I doing, darling?' she whispered. 'I don't want the poor child to be too unhappy.'

Carey gathered her remaining dignity. 'I'm terribly sorry, Michelle, but Brandon forgot to tell me you were coming to dinner. The party was just a little too much for this *Hausfrau*; I'm going to have a dinner tray in my room and spend the evening quietly. I'm sure Brandon will be delighted to have you stay anyway. Goodnight, dear.' She stood on tiptoe to brush his cheek with her kiss, and swept out of the room.

In her bedroom, she stood in front of a long mirror

staring at herself. It had all been too much today, she told herself. From Mr Fellowes and Brandon's will, through Gail's problems and the light-fingered maid—it was too much to expect anyone to handle in a day. Michelle was only the whipped cream on top of the chocolate mousse. Carey knew quite well that a good hostess never walked out on a guest, even an unexpected one, Brandon would be furious—unless he was delighted to have Michelle to himself.

And why should it upset her, no matter what he thought?

Anne was to later find Carey lying across her bed, indulging in a hearty bout of tears, when she brought her her dinner tray.

Brandon's appointments secretary, the lady of the seductive voice, said, 'Thank you for coming down, Mrs Scott.'

'I was in the neighbourhood anyway, Lisa. Tell me more about what Mr Scott has in mind.'

'Every year he gives a Christmas party for the company vice-presidents and their wives at September Hill, to kick off the Christmas season. Usually it's just cocktails and dinner, and it's always the first weekend of December. All of the menus and everything for the last umpteen years are here.' She pulled open the drawer of a filing cabinet.

Carey looked at the row of fat folders. 'I see why you asked me to come here. This year, I suppose, he'd like to do something a little different, now that he has a hostess again.'

'That's right. It's awfully short notice, I know, but you've been so busy . . .'

Carey sighed. 'Yes, it has been a wearing few weeks. Why don't you get me the last few years' records, and I'll go off in a corner with them and see if inspiration strikes.'

'Here they are. Mr Scott's gone out to one of the plants this afternoon if you'd like to use his office.'

'Am I safe till three o'clock?'

'He won't be back till late.'

'Then I will use his office, thank you. Warn me if you see him coming.'

She hadn't been in Brandon's office since the day he had proposed. If you could rightfully call it a proposal, she thought, twisting the diamond and sapphire ring on her finger. She walked slowly across the carpet and laid the folders on the small conference table. Not for anything would she risk using his desk; she would mix something up for sure and draw his anger upon her.

She unbuttoned the tweed jacket of her tailored trouser suit and draped it over a chair, thinking that he hadn't been angry with her in a week. He had blown up at her for walking out on Michelle that night, but since then he had merely been cold. Half the time he didn't even come home, and Carey assumed he was spending his time with Michelle, either at her apartment or in the famous bedroom in the penthouse office suite.

She looked up from the party plans and her eyes fell on the door that led to the apartment. Through that door was the dining room that Brandon used for the weekly luncheon with his vice-presidents. And beyond that must lay the suite that no one Carey knew of had ever seen. There were plenty of rumours about what it looked like, and even more rumours about the sort of thing that went on there.

Carey nibbled on a fingernail. It was tempting, she thought. Very, very tempting. Then she resolutely dragged her mind back to the party plans.

It didn't matter to her where Brandon spent his time, or with whom—she wasn't letting it bother her. But she did think that he could be a little more discreet for his mother's sake. Nancie was plainly worried; she had tried to reassure Carey just yesterday with the news that Michelle was scheduled to be off on another foreign assignment, this one in Tokyo.

Carey had merely shrugged. She kept telling herself that surely he wouldn't let this drag on. Surely he wouldn't keep himself tied up in a marriage that had no advantages for him when he really wanted to be with Michelle. Perhaps her freedom wasn't so far away.

Dream on, she told herself. If she was stubborn, so was he, and Carey wasn't foolish enough to think she could defeat Brandon at his own game. No one could outlast him when he had made up his mind. It was a depressing thought.

She tried to concentrate on the party plans, but her eyes kept returning to that door in the corner of the office. Finally she moved to the other side of the table so that she couldn't look at it.

She settled herself and looked up to find a new piece of art on the wall opposite her. It was a very large print of the colour photograph that had been with the newspaper story Gail had clipped for her—the picture of them dancing the last waltz at their wedding reception.

She went over to look at it closely. It almost looked like a painted canvas.

'I found some files on other company parties, Mrs Scott,' Lisa said, coming in with another stack of folders. 'Isn't that picture beautiful? I've admired it since the day Mr Scott had it hung.'

'It does look nice there,' Carey admitted.

'When will you be having your sitting?'

'My sitting?'

'I was certain they discussed . . . when the photographer was here . . . I'm sorry, I shouldn't have said anything.'

'When am I having my portrait made, you mean?' Carey tried to laugh it off. 'Perhaps Mr Scott is going to surprise me. Don't worry about ruining it; I promise to be surprised.' And she would be, she told herself. She would be shocked to tears.

Lisa seized the opening gratefully. 'That must have been it. If you need anything else, Mrs Scott, just call.'

After the door closed behind Lisa, Carey turned back to the photograph. It was good work; the young photographer had had reason for his self-confidence. Brandon must have been impressed by it, for not only had he bought this piece but apparently had arranged a sitting for someone else. One of his rare, interesting women, no doubt. Probably Michelle.

Gail was right, Carey decided; she would have a full set of formal photographs made. Every woman wanted to be immortalised. Besides, Carey thought, if she had to live like this for a year, she would be grey-haired. She would need a photograph to remember what she had looked like.

She looked up and her eyes fell again on that tempting door. This time Carey didn't hesitate. If Michelle was occupying that bedroom there would be evidence of it, and while she didn't care if Brandon was sleeping with the woman, it would give her an idea of how long this game might go on.

Her heart was pounding as she walked through the dining room and stepped into a big living room with long windows stretching from the floor to the ceiling on the far wall.

The curtains were open and the afternoon sun cast bars of light over the grey carpet. The walls were stark white, the accents in shiny black and white. Above the fireplace hung a single modern painting composed of black and white lines and a single red dot. Carey looked at it with disfavour. She was going to have to take a class in modern art appreciation, she decided. She was sure it was a good painting—Brandon would never own anything that wasn't—but it didn't do anything for her.

It was a sophisticated room, a room to entertain in but not one that looked comfortable. She couldn't imagine Brandon sitting here with his shoes off and his feet up. She dismissed the thought and walked across the room. Beyond it lay a kitchenette that looked as if it had never been used. Of course it hadn't she told herself. If Brandon wanted a cup of coffee he'd call the restaurant downstairs and have it delivered. That left only the door at the other end of the living room.

She took a deep breath. It wasn't as if she were trespassing, she told herself. She had a perfect right to be here, and she pushed open the bedroom door.

The curtains were drawn and the room was dim, and she could see only the vague outlines of the furniture. She groped for a light switch, and as her hand hit a button music swelled from concealed speakers around the room. Carey giggled. 'How convenient,' she muttered, and flipped the next switch.

Soft indirect lighting sprang to life, casting pools of light across the quilted white satin comforter that covered the king-sized bed. Matching ruffled slips encased the pillows. The bed itself was a priceless antique, carved of walnut so dark it looked almost black, the four turned posts reaching ceiling height to support an elaborately carved walnut canopy.

The walls were a dark rich red, a colour that looked like a beam of light shining through a goblet of priceless wine. The curtains were white brocade with a delicate tracery of black and red running up through the pattern.

'All it lacks is the company logo carved in the head-board,' Carey muttered. Her feet sank into the plush white carpet as she crossed to peek into the dressing room. Michelle must have been careful with her things, Carey concluded, or else Brandon was going to her apartment, for nothing feminine lay about. Or perhaps whoever took care of these rooms had orders to conceal the evidence behind closed doors.

She pulled the dressing room door shut behind her and looked at the bedroom again. It wasn't nearly as decadent as the rumours described it. There wasn't so much as a Matisse nude on the walls. Frankly, Carey decided, she was disappointed.

The room had a certain charm. She sat down on the edge of the bed and was startled as the mattress seemed to shift from under her with a gurgle. Of course, it would be a waterbed, she told herself, and fighting the giggles, lay back across the puffy comforter. Above her head was a mirror that lined the entire canopy, reflecting the whole bed. Carey stared at herself for an instant. Then she said, 'That completes it! The perfect finishing touch!' and collapsed in giggles. She laughed until she was helpless, rolling over to pound her fist on the mattress, which sloshed in protest.

'It sounds as if you're having a good time.'

Carey tried to sit up, but the waterbed wouldn't let her do so with any dignity. She rolled over and looked warily up at Brandon, who was rubbing his hair with a towel. Another towel was slung about his narrow hips and was the only thing he wore.

'You've just got out of the shower,' she stammered.

'Your powers of observation are improving,' he mocked. 'Have you ever considered becoming a private detective?'

'But they said you were out of the office.'

'I was. And then I came back. It would be useless to have an apartment up here if I couldn't get into it without my staff knowing I was here.' He came towards the bed. 'I must say it's pleasant to find you waiting for me, Carey.' His voice was rich and deep. He leaned over her, effectively pinning her to the bed without touching her at all.

'I wasn't waiting for you.' Her voice was breathless.

'But you're here, and that's all that matters.' He was beside her on the bed, his hand moving gently up the row of buttons on her waistcoat.

'You promised you'd leave me alone.'

He spread the waistcoat open, his hands warm on the thin fabric of her blouse, and shook his head. 'I said I'd stay out of your bed, and I have. I made no promises about what I'd do if I found you in mine. It looks like an invitation to me.' The buttons were undone now and he tugged gently at the big bow at her throat until it untied and the blouse fell open. He bent his head to kiss her breast. 'How thoughtful of you not to wear a bra today,' he said, his tongue teasing gently. 'Shall I try to find some hidden meaning in that?'

'I didn't plan this, that's for certain!' she said sharply, and tried to move away.

He wouldn't let go of her. 'Make love with me, Carey,' he said. 'Let me remind you of how beautiful it can be.'

'No!'

'Why not? There's nothing wrong.' He reached for her left hand and turned the wedding ring on her finger. 'Remember this? That makes it all right.'

'It's wrong to go to bed with someone you hate, no matter how many rings you wear,' she moaned, tossing her head on the satin pillowslip as his teeth nibbled their way across her shoulder and up her throat.

'I think hate is a strong word. You want me, Carey. And I want you. I want to kiss you, and touch you, and make love to you . . .'

'You'll have to rape me, then,' Carey said flatly. 'I'm not drunk this afternoon.'

'Are you trying to convince me or yourself?' But Brandon's hands were still.

She jerked out of his hold and scrambled off the bed, her hands clumsy as she frantically rebuttoned her blouse.

He stayed on the bed, stretched out lazily, his arms folded behind his head, his eyes watching her. 'Why are you in such a hurry, Carey? Are you afraid of me, or yourself?'

She didn't answer, just tucked the blouse in and started to button her waistcoat.

'I wouldn't have to use force, Carey. I didn't last time and we both know it. You're not running from me because you're afraid I'll rape you. You're running because you know I wouldn't have to, that if I came after you right now you would enjoy it when I made love to you.'

The waistcoat buttoned, Carey smoothed her hair with shaking fingers and almost ran across the room.

The deep, relentless voice pursued her to the door, 'When are you going to stop running from yourself, Carey?'

In his office, she seized her tweed jacket and a couple

of folders off of the stack on the table.

Lisa wasn't at her desk, so Carey went on through to the main reception room. Her hand was on the door when she heard a petulant voice from the outer room.

'When will Mr Scott be back?'

'I don't have any idea, Miss Lantry.' The secretary was soothing, as though she had had a lot of practice.

'Just let me wait in the living room for him, won't you?'

'I can't, Miss Lantry. No one goes into the suite unless Mr Scott is there.'

Michelle laughed. 'I've been there dozens of times. He'll be furious when he finds out you made me wait out here.'

'I'm sorry; the rule still stands.'

Carey smiled and pushed the door open. 'It's quite a sensible rule, Michelle,' she said as she crossed the reception room. 'You just never know who you might find in Brandon's apartment these days.' She didn't break step as she crossed the room, but she could feel Michelle's eyes summing up the slightly dishevelled hair and the neckline that looked as if it had been tied in a bit of a hurry.

The model's eyes had been green and hard with jealousy, Carey thought as she sank into a corner of the express elevator, feeling safe for the first time all afternoon. She smiled. Brandon might just have a hard time explaining that to Michelle. She wished that she had thought to warn the woman that jealousy was the first thing that turned him off.

She was still thinking about that as she walked through the atrium lobby. The fountain splashed into a deep pool which held dozens of enormous goldfish. Michelle had looked rather like one of those goldfish when she had seen Carey.

She was laughing at the thought when she ran head-long into Clarke Dennis.

He steadied her. 'Watch it, Carey. You'll be walking into walls next.'

'Sorry, Clarke. I didn't know you were back to work yet.'

'Neither does my doctor,' he grinned. 'Brandon's out this afternoon.'

'He's back now.' Her gaze slid from Clarke to the man at his elbow. 'Hi, Doug.'

'Good afternoon, Mrs Scott.' Doug's voice was cold and his eyes were hard. 'If you'll excuse me, Clarke.' Without waiting for an answer, he strode across the lobby and into a waiting elevator.

Carey shook her head in disbelief. 'He really is angry with me, isn't he?'

Instead of answering, Clarke asked, 'Does he have a right to be angry?'

'No, Clarke. We dated, but we were both seeing other people. Then Brandon . . .' She stopped guiltily.

'Then Brandon did what, my dear?' Clarke's voice was gentle, and for an instant Carey wanted to fling herself into his arms and sob out her frustrations. Clarke would defend her from Brandon; he'd go up there right now and probably blacken Brandon's eye. But she caught herself in time. The cost to Clarke would be high, and she couldn't do that to Clarke and Nancie.

'Then Brandon swept me off my feet, Clarke,' Carey said clearly, looking at him steadily.

Clarke studied her in silence for a moment with raised eyebrows. 'If you say so, Carey,' he said finally. 'I wanted you to look at the public relations packages you were working on and see what you think of the way Doug finished them. Do you have time?'

'I don't think that would be a good idea.'

'Perhaps you're right. Do you have a car?'

'Yes. The chauffeur is waiting. I hope Doug cools down soon. Do you think there is anything I could do?'

'Not unless you can convince him that you didn't marry Brandon for his money. And I can't imagine him being convinced.'

'There are a lot of people who think that.'

He held the door for her, and didn't say what Carey

was certain he was thinking. But it was better if Clarke thought she had seized the opportunity to marry wealth than if he knew the truth.

CHAPTER NINE

IT rained the next morning. It was still unseasonably warm, and what in other Novembers would have been snow fell steadily in torrents from a dark grey sky, punctuated with jagged streaks of lightning and thunder that pounded against her eardrums until she thought she would scream.

Storms didn't frighten Carey, but the heavy rain depressed her, and she wandered from room to room, unable to settle to anything. She finally sat down at the grand piano in the little alcove off the main drawing room and, opening the keyboard, played a few chords. The keys responded in perfect tune. 'Of course,' she muttered. 'A piano owned by Brandon Scott would never have the nerve to get out of tune.'

She ran gentle fingers up and down a scale, feeling stiffness in her fingers, long unaccustomed to playing. She wandered from one remembered favourite to another, letting memories of the past wash over her. The happiest times with her father had been the hours they spent together at the piano as he taught her to play. His love of music—along with his skill at billiards—had been his greatest charm. It had been years since she had missed him so desperately. She dropped her hands from the keyboard, her eyes filling with tears. Her father had been irresponsible with money, perhaps, but he had loved her.

Whitney came into the room, soft-footed, and watched her for a few moments. Then he said gently, 'Mrs Dennis is on the telephone, Mrs Scott.'

Carey jumped and said, 'You startled me, Whitney.'

'I'm sorry, madam.'

She caught a look of sympathy in his eyes as he turned away. She knew he was thinking that her tears were for

126

Brandon and the wreck their new marriage had so quickly become. She sat up straight. Whitney knew, as all the staff did, about the nights in the last week that Brandon had not come home at all. Most of the staff, Carey thought, were sympathetic to her. They worked for Brandon, but they didn't respect him, and when the storybook marriage went sour, they felt sorry for the abandoned wife.

She brushed tears off her long lashes and took a deep breath before going to the telephone.

'Hi, darling,' Nancie said cheerily. 'Would you like to go out for lunch today?'

'No thanks, Nancie. The rain has made me so gloomy I wouldn't be much company.'

Nancie was silent for a moment. 'Are you sure it's the rain, Carey?'

'What do you mean?'

'I know quite well that I'm rushing in where angels fear to tread, but Brandon hasn't been coming home at night lately, has he?'

Carey was silent. While she didn't go out of her way to confide in Nancie, neither would she lie to her. 'No, he hasn't,' she admitted.

Nancie's anger vibrated across the wires. 'I could just spank him!' she stormed. 'What ails the man?'

Carey sighed. 'Nancie, you know it was in the cards that this might not last very long,' she said, trying to choose her words with care.

'I was hoping that you were the woman he wanted so badly that everything else would come second.'

'I don't think that woman exists, Nancie.'

Nancie sighed unhappily. 'If you were to have a baby . . .'

'A child born into a marriage like this one wouldn't be glue to hold us together. He'd be a rubber band twisted and stretched and probably broken between us.'

'I know you're right, Carey. But Brandon loves you; I know he does. I can see it in his eyes.'

Then you're the only one who can, Carey thought,

and tried to reassure Nancie. 'I'm not going to walk out,' she said. As if I could, she added to herself. 'So if Brandon really loves me . . .' It sounded strange to say the words.

It soothed Nancie, who said, 'I guess lunch wouldn't be a good idea. We'd cry all over each other. Perhaps tomorrow, when we're both in a better mood?'

'Good idea,' Carey told her.

The rain had stopped as she sat down at the desk in her morning room and tackled the plans for the Christmas party. It might, if she was lucky, be the only one she would ever throw at September Hill, but she would make sure it was one to remember.

The sun broke through as she raised her head from writing the last item on her menu, and Carey smiled. She would stop by the Rocking Horse, she decided, and see how Gail was doing. Then she would talk to the caterers and make arrangements for her party. It didn't have to be a gloomy day, she decided. She wouldn't let it stay that way. And if she left now, she wouldn't be here for Lynne's daily phone call and litany of complaints.

She was coming down the steps with her lists, pulling on her gloves, when Whitney stopped her. 'Another telephone call, madam,' he said. 'It's Mr Scott's secretary.'

Carey took the phone. At least it wasn't Lynne, she told herself. 'Yes, Lisa?'

'Mr Scott asked me to tell you that he has invited a houseguest to stay at September Hill for a couple of days. Would you make the arrangements? The name is Tony Millhouse—a scientist working on a new product for one of the corporations, I guess.'

'All right. Thank you, Lisa.' She put the phone down and called to Whitney. When the butler reappeared, she said, 'We'll be having a houseguest for a few days. Would you make certain that the blue guest room is ready? I'll take care of the details when I get home.'

'Of course, madam.'

The Lincoln was waiting at the door. The chauffeur

helped Carey in, and she said, 'Do you know where the Rocking Horse is? On Elgin Avenue?'

'Yes, madam.' He didn't seem to wonder about why she was visiting a nursery school, Carey reflected. It wasn't his business to wonder. It was an awful temptation sometimes to see just how far she could push the servants before they would lose that implacable calm. Which just goes to prove, she told herself, that I was never intended to be a woman of means, waited on hand and foot. I'll always be a working girl.

The car pulled out into traffic and started towards the Rocking Horse. Carey hoped that she would find Gail there. Surely in these few days she wouldn't have had everything taken down and moved, even if she had found somewhere to move it to.

There was no problem with recognising the building, for two men on ladders were putting up a huge, gaily painted sign in the shape of a hobbyhorse, while Gail, in jeans, directed them from below. She came running when the Lincoln pulled up, and when Carey got out she found herself in a bear-hug.

'Carey, I don't care what you think of your husband, I think he's a pretty special guy,' Gail bubbled.

'What happened?'

'Don't you know? He got the zoning change made, and I have my licence, so I can open on schedule!'

'How do you know Brandon had anything to do with it?'

'Because my one and only friend at City Hall nosed around, and he found out that Brandon Scott himself let it be known that he would consider it a favour if the Rocking Horse opened on time.' Gail did a little jig. 'I'm so happy I could kiss him!'

'I'm sure he'd like that.' That doesn't sound like Brandon, she thought. 'Since everything is on schedule again, may I have the grand tour?'

'Of course.' Gail's laughter bubbled frequently as she walked Carey through the building, from the nursery for the little ones to the bright playrooms for the older children. The library was already stocked with books ready to be used, and even the bulletin boards were arranged with colourful pictures.

'You'll open next week, right?' Carey asked. 'Would you like some volunteer help when you get going?'

'Of course. How would you like to read to the kids— have a story hour now and then? It would make a change for them.'

'All right. Let me know when.'

'On one condition, of course; I want to meet that gorgeous man and tell him how much I appreciate his help.'

Carey was beginning to see a little light. Perhaps Brandon had reason to give Gail a boost. It certainly couldn't hurt his cause if he spent some time keeping her friends happy.

'We're having a houseguest for a few days,' Carey said. 'Perhaps you can come to dinner one night. He's a research scientist.'

'Sounds like my type.' Gail grinned.

The afternoon flew by as Carey talked to caterers, florists, and decorators, and when she started for home, she was horrified at the time. She hoped she would be home before Brandon got there, but she was too late.

When Whitney opened the door for her, he said, 'Mr Scott is in the billiard room, madam. He'd like you to go in for a moment.'

She walked down the parquet-floored hall, heels tapping. As she opened the door of the billiard room, she heard the unmistakable thunk of the ivory balls striking together. She pushed the door wide and saw Brandon, in slacks and sports shirt, his back to her, lining up another shot.

'Did you want to talk to me?'

'So you're finally home.' The tone of his voice irritated her. As if he had been around enough the past few days to know when she was there.

She glanced at the clock and perched on the arm of a chair. 'It isn't six o'clock yet. You'll notice I'm conceding the definition of home.'

Brandon ignored her. 'I asked for arrangements to be made for a houseguest.'

'They weren't? I asked . . .' No, Carey, she told herself. He's right about that; you were responsible and you shouldn't have delegated the job, even to Whitney.

'They were, but inadequately. I had to change everything around when we got here. And incidentally, it would have been pleasant to have the hostess here when we arrived.'

'Oh, it would? Then next time you'd better give me a little more notice. I don't think I ever agreed not to leave this house for the rest of my life, and I happened to be working on your party plans most of the afternoon. I had the impression it was of primary importance.'

'It is. But you could have arranged to greet your guest anyway.' He started to put his cue back into the rack.

'My guest? Since when is someone I've never seen before, and whom you invite for business reasons, *my* guest? It's been made very plain to me that I am a functionary in this house, not a partner.' She paused for a second. 'Don't stop playing on my account, by the way. I'd prefer for you to take out some of that hostility on the balls instead of on me.'

'What makes you think you're only a functionary?' He took aim at another ball. 'You're the hostess here.'

'If that isn't a functionary, I'd like to know what is!'

'Would you like to change the arrangement? I'd be delighted to oblige you.'

'And all I have to do is leave my bedroom door open? No thanks.' She put her hands on her hips. 'How am I supposed to be a hostess when you don't tell me anything in time to act on it? If I'd known yesterday I was going to have a guest, I'd have laid out the towels with my own little hands!'

Brandon was laughing. 'See? You just admitted that Tony is your guest.'

Carey stared at him for a moment, then reluctantly smiled. She had been caught out.

'I'll try to give you more notice in the future, honey. I'm used to dealing with secretaries; I'll have to break that habit. Would you like to play a game of pool?'

Carey relented. He was so fearfully charming, and it was too exhausting to stay angry. Besides, he always won the arguments in the end. 'How do you get Whitney to accept this? Isn't putting a pool table in a billiard room heresy?'

'Oh, when he's around I just call it pocket billiards. Do you play?'

'I've shot a little pool.' She hefted a cuestick, trying it out. 'It's been a long time since I've even had a cue in my hand.'

'I'm not so hot myself. I'm out of practice.'

'I don't believe that. You just sank three straight, and you were angry.'

'Pure luck,' Brandon assured her. 'Come on.'

Carey put the cue back and reached for another. 'By the way, thank you for the influence in getting Gail Britton's zoning problems solved.' It was said stiffly. She hated being under any extra obligation to him.

'You weren't supposed to know about that. No one was.'

'The zoning board leaks like a sieve.'

'I'm not crazy about her location myself. But it will serve to get her started.'

Carey found a cue to her taste and took aim for her break. Then a lilting voice behind her said, 'Hi, Brandon. I hope I'm not late. This must be Mrs Scott.'

Carey's cue slipped, and the ball rolled aimlessly half-way down the table. She turned to stare at the blonde beauty, in white slacks and a tight red top, standing in the doorway, and heard Brandon's smiling voice say, 'Carey, I'd like you to meet Tony Millhouse.'

She still didn't believe it two hours later, as she watched Brandon and Tony—who was now wearing a flame-red dinner dress that sparkled under the chandelier—laugh their way through dinner. She glanced down at her pale blue dress. It had looked lovely upstairs, but it just could not compete with that red rag across the table.

No wonder the blue room hadn't been satisfactory—it was a man's room. She wondered idly which room Brandon had arranged for Tony. There was a woman's guestroom right across the hall from his own room.

She sipped her wine and wondered how long Michelle had waited for Brandon. Had he ever relented and told the secretaries to let her come in? Or had he been too busy entertaining Tony? Poor Michelle—being relegated to the second string must be very uncomfortable for her.

'Shall we move into the drawing room for coffee?' she asked, and rose without waiting for an answer.

There was an instant of silence, then Tony laughed lightly. 'Of course, Mrs Scott. Brandon and I were just completely lost, weren't we?'

I wish you would both get lost, Carey thought crossly.

'I can certainly see why you married her, Brandon,' Tony went on. 'She's so restful that I almost forgot she was here!'

Brandon didn't wait for the coffee tray, but crossed straight to the table where his brandy decanter stood. 'Would you like some, Tony?' he asked.

'Oh, yes, Brandon, if it's all right with Mrs Scott.' She shot a simpering look at Carey.

'Why should I object? I occasionally indulge myself.' Carey sat and sipped her coffee and put a few stitches into a needlepoint chair cover. She decided she would probably have to yank it all out the next time she worked on it, though, because her stitches, like her thoughts, were uneven and tangled.

A few minutes later Tony came to lean over her shoulder. 'What are you making?' she asked. 'I always envied you women who are talented with your hands. I never could do any of that; science has always been my passion.'

Carey smiled sweetly. 'Oh, it takes no great talent to needlepoint. Anyone who can count and who has a certain amount of patience can pick it up. I've always envied you women who have the brains—the rare, interesting women who have such outstanding careers.'

Brandon frowned at her, but Carey pointedly ignored him and concentrated on her canvas. Finally, though, Tony's inane conversation wore her nerves down and she tossed the needlepoint aside. 'If you'll excuse me, I think I'll go practise a few pool shots. You seem to have given me the urge to repair my rusty skills, Brandon.'

'Would you still like a game?' he asked, with a sparkle in his eyes.

'Of course. You don't mind, do you, Tony? Perhaps you'd like to play the winner.'

Tony laughed. 'Playing the loser would be more my style. I never have been much good at competitive games.'

Unless you count going after a man as a competitive game, Carey thought, and scolded herself for losing control of her thoughts.

'I'll just run up to get those statistics I was telling you about, Brandon,' Tony added. 'I'll be back down in a little while.'

Carey was chalking her cue when Brandon said, 'It wasn't necessary for you to be catty to Tony. She has a few idiosyncracies, but she's one of the best people around when it comes to plastics.'

'I venture to guess her morals are plastic, too. We're playing regular eight-ball, I presume?'

'Unless you prefer something else. Would you care to place a small wager on this game?'

'What did you have in mind?'

'How about a whole day of you treating me like a human being?'

'As long as it's only the daytime hours,' Carey retorted. 'I think I'd like a diamond bracelet.'

'That's no small stake.'

'Neither is yours. Besides, I said it had been a long time since I played, and you've been practising.'

'All right. Your break.'

Carey watched him rack the balls. 'I'll take stripes,' she announced as he lifted the rack off the triangle of balls.

'Shouldn't you wait till you see if you can put any in the pockets?'

She didn't answer right away, but fired the cue ball into the triangle. 'Why waste time?' she asked reasonably as a striped ball dropped into the corner pocket.

'I think I've been conned,' Brandon announced.

Carey ignored the interruption. 'I wasn't being catty about Tony, anyway,' she said. Another striped ball teetered into a pocket. 'I didn't say a word I didn't mean. She is rare. And interesting. Didn't you think so?' Another ball dropped.

Tony came in then, so Brandon couldn't answer. Carey smiled and lined up the next shot. She put the remaining four stripes in the pockets in three shots. As she lined up the eight ball, Brandon complained, 'I thought you said you'd shot a little pool!'

Carey looked up, an amused gleam in her eyes. 'I'm a fast learner. Eight in the side pocket.'

Brandon racked his cue unused, not even watching as the ball dropped into the pocket. 'I've been hustled.'

'What did you lose?' Tony asked avidly.

'Make it a nice diamond bracelet,' Carey recommended.

'I'll play you double or nothing,' he offered. 'If you'll accept a handicap.'

'Such as?'

'Playing left-handed.'

'I'll play you one-handed if you like. But I make it a rule never to bet on the second game.'

'I'd be afraid of you, even one-handed,' Brandon admitted.

'You should be. I'm actually better that way, when I'm in practice. I'll say goodnight now, Tony, if you don't mind being left to Brandon's care.'

'Oh, not at all,' Tony assured her.

I'll bet that's the first truthful thing she's said all night, Carey thought.

Tony continued, 'Where did you learn to play like that? You could give exhibitions.'

Carey smiled at Brandon with real warmth for the first time all evening. This should give him a turn, she thought. 'At my father's knee. He was a professional pool shark. Goodnight.'

The fun of besting Brandon in front of his interesting woman friend didn't last the night. Carey woke early the next morning in a temper and lay restless, unable to go back to sleep. She rolled over and propped her chin on her hands, staring out the window, wondering if Brandon had spent the night in his own bed or in Tony's. Probably Tony's, she thought, and it made her angry. If he had to have women like Tony and Michelle around, why did he bring them to Carey to entertain?

Anne came in then, and Carey stretched lazily and pushed the blankets back. 'Anne, how do you always know the moment I wake up?'

'It comes with experience. Would you like breakfast right away, or your bath?'

'Breakfast, please.'

Anne brought the chiffon and lace robe that matched the gown Carey was wearing. 'That's what I thought. Whitney will be bringing it up any moment.'

Carey laughed. 'Do I at least have time to brush my hair?' She watched the maid's sure hands in the mirror. 'You frighten me sometimes because you have things so well under control, Anne. And you never let me out of your sight. But I really enjoy having you around.'

'Thank you, Mrs Scott. Do you want your hair back in the snood?'

'No, just leave it loose.' She studied the chestnut curls draping around her shoulders. 'I think I might cut my hair, Anne.'

'It would be a shame. And I think Mr Scott would be very angry.'

Carey ran her hands through the long strands, thinking that Anne's comment had just given her hair the kiss of death. If it would make Brandon angry, it would be worth it, she thought.

She was thinking about that and wondering if she would like having her hair short as she walked into the sitting room and saw Whitney serving scrambled eggs on to Brandon's plate. Brandon himself was just coming in, still settling his necktie into place.

'Good morning,' she said, determined to sound casual.

His eyes swept appreciatively over the thin peignoir and the long loose hair. 'I'll have to time my breakfast more carefully in the future.'

'I expected you to be gone by now.'

'It got to be a late night.'

'Your toast, madam,' Whitney said, lifting the cover off of the plate in front of her. 'And your melon. Will that be all?'

'Yes, thank you, Whitney. I'll pour the coffee.' Carey picked up her spoon trying not to look self-conscious. 'Do you have breakfast up here often?'

'Just about every day. I, too, dislike the dining room. If you'd like to do something drastic to it after Christmas, I'm in favour.'

Carey's heart jolted. He obviously intended that she would still be here after Christmas. Well, she hadn't expected anything else, had she?'

'I must say,' he continued, 'it's much more pleasant to have company.'

'If you're wondering, I'm usually dressed by the time I come to breakfast.'

'What a pity.'

Carey could feel herself flushing under his appreciative glance. 'I expected you to have breakfast with Tony.'

'She isn't up. And she opted for a tray in bed, anyway.'

'In that case, I'm really surprised that you didn't join her.'

Brandon sighed and reached for his newspaper, folded neatly beside his plate. 'I'd almost forgotten that I lost the bet last night. I wonder what it would be like to have you actually be civil to me for a whole day.'

Carey took a bite of her melon and studied her plate. The cream flowers on the white china swam a little in front of her eyes. She straightened the red rose in the bud vase that matched the breakfast set and reached for the coffee-pot. 'I deserved that,' she said mildly.

'You certainly did.' He didn't look up from the financial section.

'So why don't you try being civil to me? Would you like coffee?'

'Please. Just sugar.' He put the paper aside. 'Shall we both try to be civilised? Perhaps it will make it easier.'

'If it's so difficult to live with me, why don't you just let me go away?'

He shook his head, his eyes holding hers over the rim of his cup.

'What would you do if I just left?' Carey asked curiously.

'Come and get you. That's not a threat, Carey—that's a promise.'

She sighed. Then she said, 'In that case, do I get the diamond bracelet?'

'It depends. Was your father really a pool hustler?'

'Actually he made more money playing the piano.'

'I think I would have liked him.'

'He was totally likeable. Also totally unreliable.'

'Is that why you feel so responsible for what happens to Lynne?'

'I suppose so.'

'Be careful, Carey, that she doesn't land you in something you can't handle.'

'She landed me in this, didn't she? What could be worse?'

He looked at her steadily. 'Your tongue just has a natural sharp edge, doesn't it? Watch out that you don't turn into a shrew. Right now you're pretty enough to get away with it; you may not always be so fortunate.' He tossed his napkin down. 'Besides, it's true. You're living in a mansion, with a butler, a staff, and a personal maid, with charge accounts at every shop in town—and do you ever know how to use them!—and a private income three times what you were earning before. What could be worse?' He flung his jacket over his arm and left the room.

The conversation was still on Carey's mind as she went downstairs that morning. She wished that she understood the way Brandon's mind worked, that she could figure out why he would not let her go. The game wasn't fooling anyone. If Nancie, who so desperately wanted to believe that they were happily in love, was beginning to see below the surface, who could they be fooling?

She put the question aside and turned her attention to the daily labour going on to keep September Hill looking its best. It was funny, she thought, how she had a sixth sense about how the house was functioning. Without ever seeing any of the maids at work, she could still tell almost exactly where they were.

She flipped through the stack of mail that lay on the silver tray on the corner of her desk, and carried most of it, along with the leather case full of writing supplies, into the glassed-in solarium. This room, which opened to both terrace and pool, would probably be her favourite all winter, she thought. The flagstone floor radiated heat absorbed from the sun's rays striking down through the glass wall. The green plants loved the warmth and humidity, and so did Carey.

She stretched out in a lounge chair and reached for the tiny silver letter opener from the fitted case.

'Boy, don't you have it made.'

Carey sighed and put the opener aside. 'Hello, Lynne.'

'It must be rough, sitting out here in the sun reading while the rest of us have to work all of the time.' Lynne flung herself down on a lounger.

'I hate to be quarrelsome, but if you were working you wouldn't be here, Lynne. What do you need this morning?'

'I came out here to ask you one more time, as my sister, to persuade Brandon to put David and me back on his personal plane.'

'I can't do it, Lynne. Brandon has made up his mind that he doesn't want you on that plane.'

'But David's turn was coming up. And it's easy duty; we could be together. You could persuade him, Carey!'

'No, I couldn't. Believe me, Lynne.'

'Won't you ask him? Just ask him, that's all!'

'I won't ask him, Lynne. Isn't it enough that you got yourself into trouble the last time you were on that plane?'

'I didn't get myself into trouble. Somebody framed me. Somebody who didn't want me to take her job.'

Carey looked her sister over, then asked coolly, 'Do you have anyone specific in mind, or is that just a general accusation?'

'If you're asking me who did it, I don't know. But plenty of people on that crew didn't want me to have a job, and I want to show them.'

'I know.' Carey's voice was dry.

'What's the matter with you, Carey? You've got so sarcastic now I hardly know you. You ought to watch out; it isn't flattering.'

Carey was tempted to tell her sister that living with Brandon Scott would make a saint sarcastic, but she didn't. It was evident, however, that if the venom she felt towards him was spilling over on to other people, it was time to get herself under control before the cattiness took over her personality entirely.

Whitney came in with a tall glass of fruit juice on a silver tray. He presented the tray to Lynne, who took the glass and said, 'Well, if you won't do that for me, Carey, just that one little thing . . .'

'I won't.'

Whitney, with always-perfect manners, asked, 'Will

there be anything else, madam?'

'Just another cup of coffee when you have time,' Carey said. 'Thank you, Whitney.'

Lynne tasted the juice. 'Whitney, tell them to put some sugar in it next time. This is sour. I found the wedding gown I want yesterday at Donalan's, Carey. Will you buy it for me?'

Whitney's control was superb, but it wasn't quite good enough because Carey saw his eyebrows raise as he left the room. Whitney waited on Lynne, as the entire staff did, because she insisted on being attended hand and foot. But that didn't mean he had to like the way she treated him, or how she acted towards her sister.

Carey reached for her coffee cup. 'I'd be delighted to consider your gown my wedding gift to you.'

'Oh, Carey, don't be such a cheapskate. You're rolling in money. Besides, if I get my dress, maybe David will set a date soon.'

'Hasn't he?' Maybe David has more sense than I gave him credit for, Carey thought, if he is having second thoughts about marrying Lynne.

'No. He said we'd set it when he got back from his fishing trip in the fall. But he didn't say anything more about it when he came home.'

'Perhaps if you weren't sleeping with him, he'd be more interested in getting married.' She sipped the dregs of her coffee, thinking that Lynne was growing to be a bore. In the last few months she seemed to be getting more childish by the day.

'Don't lecture me, Little Miss Prim. You won't convince me that you're so innocent. Brandon isn't the type who buys without trying out the merchandise.'

And she's becoming crude, too, Carey thought. Or was it a change in herself?

Lynne went on, 'David says we can't afford to get married right now. We'll both have to work, of course. That's why it would be so perfect for us both to be on that plane. Then we could be together all of the time.'

'No, Lynne.'

Lynne sighed heavily. 'He's the only thing in the world I want, Carey. I'm afraid if he doesn't marry me soon he never will.' Her enormous blue eyes pleaded for her sister's help.

'Perhaps that's the way it's intended to turn out, Lynne.'

'How can you say such a rotten thing?' Lynne flared.

'What a gorgeous, peaceful place to spend the morning!' Tony's voice was cheerful as she spoke from the doorway, apparently unaware of the currents of the conversaion she had interrupted. She was dressed in tight-fitting emerald green slacks and a matching sweater, and she looked great.

She must have slept well, Carey thought, and sighed. Brandon certainly hadn't denied spending the night with the woman. No wonder she looked so contented this morning, like a kitten that had been played with to its heart's content. And again the anger Carey had felt on awakening stirred. She certainly didn't care if Brandon had a hundred women. But did he have to bring them under the same roof with his wife and expect her to keep them entertained when he was busy with other things?

'Did you sleep well, Tony?' she asked, once more the perfect hostess.

'Oh, wonderfully. I don't think I told you last night, Carey, how grateful I am that you took me in on such short notice. It was so generous of you.' Her voice was just a touch breathless, like that of an *ingénue*.

Including the loan of my husband? For an instant, Carey thought she might actually have spoken the words. 'Not at all, Tony,' she said politely. 'This is my sister, by the way—Lynne Forsythe.'

The two women exchanged nods. Lynne looked put out, which was nothing new. Tony seemed to dismiss the younger woman immediately. 'I'd be so proud if I were you, Carey,' she said. 'Some day I'm going to have a house just like this one.'

Another threat? Carey wondered what Tony's response would be if she said, 'I wouldn't count on owning September Hill, dear—there are several women already ahead of you on line.'

Tony sat down, slowly and gracefully, and stretched her legs out. 'Oh, this is splendid,' she murmured, luxuriating in the sunshine.

Lynne made frantic motions behind Tony's back. Carey ignored her sister, thinking that while entertaining a woman like Tony Millhouse wasn't exactly her first choice of pleasant pastimes, it was better than having to listen to Lynne plead and complain.

Whitney came back with a fresh pot of coffee. 'That young photographer is here to see you, madam,' he added.

'Show him into my morning room, please.'

Tony sat up. 'Are you having your portrait done? That sounds like fun, Carey.' Her tone was indulgent, as if she were talking to a child who had a silly idea. How very gauche, she seemed to be thinking, to arrange to have one's own portrait made. Her wide blue eyes swept over Carey. Especially you, they seemed to say. Who would want it?'

Carey passed it off lightly. 'I thought I'd look into it. If you will excuse me for a few minutes, Tony?'

'Of course. I really need to get some work done myself so that I'm ready to talk about it when Brandon comes home.'

Carey raised an eyebrow, but she didn't comment on her feeling that Tony was starting to act like the mistress of the house. Which, she told herself emphatically, was still quite a lot different from being the mistress of the owner of the house.

Lynne got up too. 'I need to get back to work,' she said, and followed Carey out of the room. 'What is that hussy doing here?' she asked as the solarium door closed behind them. 'She had some nerve to barge in like that.'

So did you, Carey thought. 'She's a houseguest here— a business associate of Brandon's.'

'What kind of business, that's what I'd like to know. How long will she be here?'

'I have no idea. She's Brandon's guest.'

'How innocent can you be, Carey?' Lynne's voice was contemptuous. 'Send her packing, or you'll find yourself out in the cold. You're going to have to work to keep that man, you know.'

Carey refused to be drawn. 'Was there anything else, Lynne?'

'Well—it's kind of an embarrassing question. But David and I got to talking about it, and I thought someone had better ask you. Have you ever thought about buying some life assurance or anything? I mean, you are worth a lot more now than you used to be.'

Especially to you, Carey thought, and then squashed it as an unworthy thought. She had raised Lynne to be a selfish woman; what point was there in getting upset with her now? And she could see Lynne's point. It would be only sensible to get a will made, and to make some provision for her sister. Even though she wasn't nearly as well off as Lynne thought, the income from her trust fund would add up, and she would rather Lynne have it than for Brandon to get it back, if something should happen to her.

'I'll think about it, Lynne. In the meantime, I do have a gentleman waiting for me.'

'I can take a hint. After all, everybody is more important to you than your sister is, right?' And Lynne was gone down the long hall before Carey could find an answer.

CHAPTER TEN

THE sun poured in through the glass roof of the pool house, deliciously warm on Carey's almost bare back, and the rocking motion of the air-mattress as the ripples nudged it had almost put her to sleep. Carey lay, dreamily soaking up the warmth and deciding that there were, indeed, worse fates than being Mrs Brandon Scott floating in the swimming pool on a brilliantly blue—but chilly—last day of November. In the solar-heated pool, though, it felt like June.

Of course, she told herself, one of the worst things about it was being Mrs Brandon Scott anywhere and at any time when the master of the house was present, but she wasn't going to let that bother her just now.

The last month had slid by easily. She had been busy, almost hectically so at times, and that made it easier to accept the knowledge that she would not be free to leave at any time soon. Lynne was sill persisting in her demand to be put back on to the executive jet, and Carey was still steadfastly refusing to pass the request along.

Brandon was still spending many of his nights away from September Hill. Tony had long since returned to the West Coast, but Michelle was back from Tokyo. Carey didn't know if Brandon was seeing her now, or someone else, but she knew there must be someone. Brandon was not the kind of man who would ever find himself without a woman. As long as he was leaving her alone, she told herself, she didn't care who he entertained.

Her raft bumped into the edge of the pool, so she paddled herself back out into the middle. It was pleasant to have a day to herself after the hectic activity of the last few weeks.

Having Tony around for several days had not improved Carey's temper, and it wasn't until the blonde had gone back to California that Carey had begun to feel at ease again. And then the young photographer had followed her around for the next week, the first two days to analyse her expressions, he had said, and then five full days when she had felt like an underpaid, but over-worked, model, the most photographed woman outside Hollywood. But that was all over, and now all she had to do was wait for the proofs to come back. In the mean-time, she was free to be lazy beside the pool.

Maybe she should make more of an effort to be decent to Brandon, she thought. After all, it was a very pleasant existence she was leading these days, when he wasn't there. The shock seemed to have diminished as she settled into her new routine, and it was now almost comfortable.

Carey turned over to let her stomach baste in the sun. It was a pleasure to be able to loaf in the pool on a day when she would have had to be working, and to be able to get out in a few minutes and go to Gail's grand opening celebration without asking permission from a boss. Or to shop, if she liked, without ever looking at a price tag. Yes, being married to Brandon did have its advantages. And as long as he was keeping his word about staying away from her bedroom, perhaps she should make an effort to ease the strain between them.

She dived off the raft and started to swim laps. Too many fancy dinners were having their effect, and as she pulled herself out of the pool she was breathing hard. Anne was just coming out of the solarium.

'Mrs Scott, Miss Forsythe is on the phone. She says it's urgent.'

'Bother the girl,' Carey said. 'Everything is always urgent to Lynne. What time is it?'

'Nearly two. You should be dressing for Miss Britton's grand opening.'

'Tell Lynne I'll call her back in a few minutes, after I've had a shower. Then you can at least be doing my hair while she talks.'

And it was a good thing that she had done it that way,

Carey concluded fifteen minutes later, for Lynne's call was just another of her daily hysterical outbursts.

When Carey got the story untangled, she had to admit that she was a little shocked herself. For what Lynne was telling her was that she had been visited by the ubiquitous attorney, Mr Fellowes, with orders from his client, Brandon Scott—orders that Lynne was not to contact her sister again.

'And what I want to know,' Lynne exploded, 'is where that lousy S.O.B. gets off with telling me that I can't even call you!'

'Are you certain you understood him, Lynne? I can't imagine that Brandon would do that.' But she could believe it. Brandon had no reason to like Lynne's behaviour, or to want her in his home. But Carey just couldn't understand why he would present it to Lynne in that fashion. Brandon had far more finesse than that. 'Are you positive that he said you weren't to call me?'

'I couldn't be more positive if he'd engraved it on the end of my nose. "You may not call your sister if . . ."' Lynne broke off. 'It was very plain.'

If—what, Carey wondered. There was no doubt more to this story; Lynne was not known for telling everything she knew, especially the part that wasn't to her credit.

'I'll talk to Brandon about it,' she promised. 'I'm sure you misunderstood something, Lynne.'

'Well, this is crummy, that's sure,' Lynne spat. 'And I won't put up with him telling me what I can and can't do.'

Carey found a bit of humour in the fact that Lynne's wealthy brother-in-law was obviously no longer a hero to her. 'I have to go now, Lynne. I have an appointment. But I will talk to Brandon.'

She almost had to hang up on Lynne. Thoughtfully, she watched as Anne arranged the last glossy braid of her hair. 'Anne, why would Mr Scott tell my sister not to call me?'

Anne was silent, concentrating on the last few hairpins. Then she said calmly, 'I wouldn't know, madam.

He doesn't confide in me.' She held out a small square box wrapped in silvery paper. 'This was delivered a few minutes ago.'

Carey let the subject drop, and ripped the paper off the package. Inside the velvet case, a slim, dainty diamond bracelet winked up at her.

'Oh, how lovely!' Anne exclaimed, and helped her to put it on. 'And how thoughtful of Mr Scott.'

Carey murmured, 'I thought he'd forgotten.' It had been more than three weeks since he had lost that bet. She hadn't been surprise that no diamond bracelet had been forthcoming, for she had wheedled him into the bet unfairly.

She glanced at the card and smiled ruefully. He wasn't being thoughtful, she decided. The card said, 'Even when I'm hustled, I always honour my bets eventually.'

Reluctantly, she unclasped the bracelet and put it back in the box. Was it only a coincidence that it had been delivered today? 'It's beautiful, but hardly the thing for the occasion,' she said, and handed it to Anne to put away. 'I think any jewellery would be excessive.'

She was halfway down the staircase when Whitney's voice from the front door stopped her.

'Sir, Mrs Scott is not at home to visitors today,' he was saying firmly.

'Oh, come on, old thing. From your tone of voice I know she's here. Besides, the chauffeur is waiting outside, and from previous acquaintance I'm dead sure it isn't the man of the house who's home at this time of the afternoon. Just tell Mrs Scott there's someone come to see his Princess, that's all I ask.'

'Elliot!' Carey ran down the rest of the steps.

'Thanks,' Elliot told Whitney dryly and stepped around him. 'My God, Princess, you're even prettier.' He swept her hand up to his lips.

'You've been back to France, I see,' she said, retrieving her hand.

'Only the French embassy. It was all I could afford. I nearly pined away after you left me, you know. I tried to drown your memory in brandy, but your memory is a fantastic swimmer. So—here I am.'

'I'm glad to see you.'

'You look ravishing. I'm disappointed, actually. In all of my dreams, you looked ravished instead, and you threw yourself into my arms with tears of joy. Actually, it looks as if your husband hasn't even been beating you.'

'Elliot, you haven't changed a bit.'

'Well, no. So I'll have to find new grounds for challenging him to a duel. Will he choose swords or pistols, do you think? Don't worry, I'll think of some way to protect myself.'

'You always do.'

'You're going out, I see. Shall I come along so we can get out of this nest of spies and plot our conspiracy in secret? Or is the occasion only for women?'

'You could come, but I'm not so sure you'd enjoy yourself. I'm visiting a child-care centre.'

Elliot looked doubtful. 'So why are you going? I don't see little ones tugging at your skirt, do I? And by the way, that's a very attractive skirt.' He walked around her, inspecting. 'And a very attractive . . .'

Carey cut him short. 'Thank you, Elliot, that will do. The owner is my best friend, so I have to be there when she starts this new venture.'

'Your best friend? Is she anything like you?'

'I don't know. Not physically, at least. She's red-haired, and shorter than I am . . .'

'Like so?' Elliot held a hand at his own chin level.

'Just about.'

'And like so?' He sketched a shapely figure in the air.

'Pretty close, but Elliot . . .'

'Then let's go. Face it, Princess, if your husband isn't going to beat you, you can't expect me to hang around for ever. I have to be off looking for a new damsel in distress.' He swept her out to the car, and Carey caught a glimpse of Whitney's face, and thought his calm was probably shattered for ever.

The grand opening was a great success, and Gail

looked her most beautifully professional as she greeted her prospective clients' parents. Carey found herself pressed into service reading stories, and Elliot disclosed a totally unexpected talent for creating games that no one had ever heard of before.

After the last guests departed, Gail came into the playroom where Carey and Elliot had spent the afternoon, flung herself into a beanbag chair and said, with her eyes closed, 'I now have a total of thirty-seven little darlings signed up, starting next Monday morning. Does anybody want a job?'

'Yes,' Elliot said brightly.

'You're joking.' Gail didn't even open her eyes.

'No. I'm looking forward to telling my mother that I'm giving up my studies to become a babysitter. It should be an interesting reaction.'

'Elliot, don't tease the poor girl. Are you ready to go? Why don't both of you come to dinner?'

'Are you sure Brandon won't mind?' Gail asked. 'It's awfully sudden.'

'He probably won't be there. He hasn't been home for dinner once this week. And he'd better not mind, anyway. He's the one who brought the houseguest home on two hours' notice.'

'Oh, yes, I never got to meet the houseguest,' Gail said. 'Was he as fantastic as you expected?'

'He turned out to be a she, and since I'd prepared a man's guest room, it was a panic.'

Gail looked regretful. 'I'm going to mourn the passing of that tall, dark and handsome scientist. I think I'd already fallen in love.'

'She was tall, and definitely handsome. But not your type at all, Gail. Are you coming to dinner?'

'If you're sure that Brandon won't mind. I don't want to cause any problems.'

'Why worry about him?' Elliot demanded. 'The Princess has commanded. I'll pick you up at seven, Tadpole.'

'Tadpole?' Carey asked on the way home. 'Why Tadpole?'

'Because she flits, just like a tadpole. They're never where you expect them to be. And besides, she's just a little tad. You told me she'd come up to here on me. Actually it was only to here.' He looked at Carey reproachfully.

'Usually she wears higher heels,' Carey said, and suddenly realised how utterly ridiculous the whole conversation was.

'Ah! That explains it. I'm glad that you are once again established as being reliable.' The car pulled up outside Elliot's hotel, and he said, 'Until seven-thirty, Princess,' with a heartbroken look that said he doubted he'd live that long without her.

'Oh, get out, Elliot,' Carey said not unkindly. He smiled at her—a gentle, forgiving smile—and got out.

Anne clasped the diamond bracelet around Carey's wrist, and Carey turned her hand back and forth in front of the mirror, admiring the sparkle and thinking about what she wanted to say to Brandon about the accusations Lynne had made that afternoon. There was a tap at her dressing room door and he came in, looking taller than ever and very formidable in severely styled formal clothes.

'Hi, Brandon,' she said cheerfully. 'The bracelet is lovely. Thank you!'

He didn't spare it a glance. 'Enjoy your trophy. Unlike you, I pay my bills even when I'm not told the whole truth in advance.'

'Ouch.' Carey didn't look at him. 'Lynne called me today, complaining about you.'

'I see. Fellowes must have finally caught her at home.' He perched on the corner of her dressing table and watched as Anne smoothed the last few hairs up into the elaborate twist.

'I'm glad you didn't deny it. She told me she'd been forbidden to call me again.' Carey glanced at him furtively in the mirror.

He folded his arms across his broad chest. 'Fellowes told her she could call you any time as long as she stopped bringing up the subject of money.'

'I wondered if that might be it,' Carey murmured. 'I hardly think that was necessary, Brandon.'

'Oh? I gathered that it was very necessary. Little Lynne talks of nothing else, and it seems to be uncomfortable for you to tell her to stop it.'

'I don't take kindly to your interference in my relationship with my sister.'

He shrugged. 'Take it however you like—I'll do as I please about Lynne. Right now it pleases me to eliminate her little games. If I have to set up a trust fund for her, to do the trick, I will. And speaking of trouble-spots, I hear the whippersnapper is having dinner with us.'

'Yes. He dropped in this afternoon and took me to Gail's open house.' She tipped her eyelashes with another coat of mascara. 'And if you are upset by what you call troublespots, why don't you just . . .' She stopped because Anne was there, waiting to finish styling her hair.

'Divorce you? No, thanks. Don't be shocked, Carey. After all, we haven't been fooling Anne either. How did the open house go?'

'It was beautiful, Brandon. A really stunning success. I also invited Gail to dinner to celebrate.'

'Why don't we go out for the evening? Dinner and the theatre perhaps? Then I won't have to listen to Elliot all evening.'

'You never did listen to Elliot. You were always dancing with Michelle.' Carey knew better than to ask how he could get tickets at such short notice. 'And Mrs Whitney would kill if we went out so suddenly.'

'You're probably right. We'll have dinner here and go out later.'

'Splendid.' She glanced at him in the mirror, the dark hair curling crisply down over the edge of his collar, the well-tailored dinner coat and brilliant white pleated shirt, and said almost diffidently, putting her resolution of that morning into effect, 'Have I ever told you how nice you look in evening clothes?'

He glanced over his shoulder. 'No. Why is it that I expect to find an assassin creeping up behind me?' Then he smiled. 'I'm sorry, Carey. It was an irresistible impulse. Are you going to be ready soon?'

'Just another minute,' Anne said tartly. 'If she'll sit still that long.'

Brandon stood up. 'I'll tell Whitney we'll be going out. By the way, I'd also like to ask you not to make any other arrangements for Lynne—no life assurance policies naming her as the beneficiary, or anything of that sort.'

'Why not?'

'Just call it superstition.' He walked out, whistling.

Carey sat silent for an instant. 'Well! I wonder what that was all about.'

'Probably nothing for you to worry about,' Anne advised. 'Is madam's hair satisfactory?'

Carey was so preoccupied that she didn't even notice what Anne had called her. 'I can't imagine Lynne telling Mr Fellowes that I'd been checking into life assurance. I wonder how Brandon found out.' And it was irritating that he would give no better reason than "superstition". She was willing to bet that Brandon Scott didn't know what superstition was. But at least he had asked instead of ordered; that was progress of a sort.

Elliot was in top form by dessert time, entertaining Gail and Carey impartially. They sat at the edge of the main dining area of one of the most exclusive restaurants in the city, and Elliot looked out over the crowd and wickedly described the imaginary personal lives of those sitting nearby. He was hilarious, and even Brandon was amused now and then, however reluctantly.

Finally Elliot decided to turn serious, and said, 'This was a great idea, Brandon—dinner at home and dessert out. I just might get into the nightclub business and offer this as a service. The little lady can tell her husband he doesn't have to take her out for dinner, just for some ice cream. Then before he knows it, here he is. Yes, I might do that after my present occupation loses its charm.'

'Exactly what is your present occupation?' Gail asked.

Elliot looked injured. 'Don't you recognise me? I'm a professional whatever-comes-along. Right now, I'm going to be a professional babysitter.'

'Are you really? I thought you were kidding.'

'If the pay is right. Carey said she'd volunteer, so you can give me her salary too.'

Under cover of the wage negotiations, Brandon leaned over to whisper in Carey's ear. 'That boy could sell sandboxes to sheiks,' he murmured. 'By the way, I like your Gail.'

Did he think she was a rare, interesting woman? Carey wished suddenly that she hadn't dreamed up the plans for this evening.

'I'll get the real estate people looking for a more suitable location for her business. That neighbourhood will be going downhill soon.'

'Do you always know these things in advance?'

'If I did, they'd elect me President. I think I prefer to stay in the less democratic organisation. Did you volunteer to help Gail?'

'Yes.' She looked at him warily. 'Just to read to the kids once a week or so.' She toyed with the diamond bracelet. 'So many of them, even from good homes, are never read to. And they need that contact.' She broke off, suddenly realising that she was beginning to lecture. It might not be prudent to share her views on child-raising, which were many, with Brandon. Up to now she had had him convinced that children in general were loathsome to her.

He looked at her closely, and drew a breath as if to answer, but the waiter brought their desserts just then.

'I didn't think an elegant place like this would actually serve you a double chocolate sundae,' Gail told Elliot.

'Why wouldn't they? Brandon's money is just as good as the next guy's. It's probably better, actually. We got a table, didn't we?'

'But of that whole dessert menu, the only thing you wanted was ice cream?'

'Honey, you have no idea. Europe is a wasteland. What good are all the gourmet chefs if they don't know what chocolate ice cream should taste like? I came home from France with a craving that will take a year to fill up.' He dug into his sundae with relish.

Gail gave up. 'And you—' she turned accusingly to Brandon. 'You just sit there and drink coffee and watch the rest of us consume all these calories . . .'

Brandon smiled. 'It's Irish coffee, Gail; it's hardly as innocent as you make it sound.'

'But hardly as guilty as crêpes Suzette and cherries jubilee.'

'That's true,' Elliot chimed in. 'And how you can sit there and enjoy watching those poor crêpes burn to death, Tadpole . . .'

'Are you terribly bored now that you aren't working, Carey?' Brandon asked quietly. He stirred his coffee.

'Not really. But all my life I've had a job, and now that I don't . . .'

'All your life?'

Carcy smiled. 'It seems that way. Taking care of Lynne, making sure Daddy got to work on time, when he had work . . .'

'Trying to make the money stretch?' he asked gently. 'You've been taking care of other people for so long. Why don't you relax and let someone take care of you for a change?'

His gentleness came as a shock to her, and instead of answering flippantly, Carey said softly, 'I think I've forgotten how.'

'Let me teach you.' There was an instant of silence between them. 'Let's go dance, Carey. Don't let us interrupt your argument, Elliot.' His tone was dry.

'I don't allow anything to interrupt a good argument,' Elliot said cheerfully and returned to the attack.

They hadn't danced together in weeks. Carey was

surprised to find herself comfortable in his arms, as though the strain of the last few weeks had all gone away. She found herself thinking that it was the first time since their wedding day that she had had all of his attention. Even the few evenings they had spent alone together his mind had been on business.

The music was slow and sensuous, and Carey let her head drop on to Brandon's shoulder. They danced as they had at their wedding, moving as one person.

He really was a marvellous dancer, she thought, letting her eyes close dreamily. Even the overbearing manner he had sometimes abated as he danced. His hands were firm, but he was sensitive to every nuance of his partner's movements. He had been as considerate a lover as he was a dancer, she thought, remembering their wedding night with—was it longing? For the first time she realised that she would like it if he wanted to make love to her again.

Her feet were suddenly leaden. Brandon tightened his clasp. 'Are you all right?' he asked.

'Yes, I just stumbled.' She was scarcely aware of what she said. The piercing knowledge that had just burst upon her had almost made her forget where she was.

How long had she been in love with her husband?

Was that why she had always felt so awkward when he was near her, as if she was about to trip over her own feet? Was that why she was nervous every time he put an arm around her or dropped a casual kiss on her cheek for the benefit of those around them? Did she resent him so because he had not insisted on his right to share her bed—because he had rejected her so quickly?

She didn't know how much time had gone by when she felt a curtain brush her shoulder and heard the music grow fainter. She opened her eyes to find herself in a small dim room off the dance floor.

'Do you always know where the secluded alcoves are?' she murmured.

'Always. It comes in handy for things like this.'

It was a long, gentle kiss. Had he read her mind, Carey

wondered vaguely, even as she seemed to dissolve in his arms, her body moulding against his until there seemed to be no distinction between them. She let her hands run gently up his arms and across the broad shoulders, her fingertips seeking out the crisply curling hair at the back of his neck.

He lifted his head and said unsteadily, 'My God, Carey, if I ever call you the Ice Maiden again you can slap me.'

Carey ignored his words and tugged his head down until his mouth met hers again. He sighed deep in his throat, a sigh that was more like a moan, and pulled her even closer, his lips growing more demanding as they parted hers and tasted the sweetness of her mouth.

Much later, he held her a fraction of an inch away from him and said, 'Carey—would it be so hard to give me what I want?'

A bolt of lightning stabbed through her rosy-pink cloud and an ominous peal of thunder followed as she realised what he meant.

'A child?' she asked faintly.

'Yes. That's all I want, Carey.'

She stiffened and pushed him away. In the glow of her newly-discovered love, she had forgotten that Brandon didn't share that feeling. All he wanted from her was the loan of her body—and he wouldn't want that if he didn't need help to create his precious son. Once his child was born, he would soon be rid of the encumbrance the mother of that child would be to him. Her voice trembled. 'There isn't anything you wouldn't stoop to, to get what you want!'

'What's the matter with you? You kiss me like that, then all of a sudden I'm holding an icicle again. Is what I want so unreasonable? You're my wife . . .'

'But I'm not your—your brood mare! You made me marry you; all right, I'm a prisoner. But you cannot force me to bring another human life into this misery! My children will be born of love, not of a wish to see a dynasty continued, or an experiment in crossbreeding!'

He started to speak. 'Carey—'

She stumbled on. 'If that's what you want, I'm amazed that you chose to honour me. My I.Q. is only average. Why not talk to one of your rare, interesting women friends? I'm sure at least one would be interested. Maybe you could even start a competition!' She whirled to leave the alcove, but he caught her arm in a fierce grip. 'Let me go!' she cried.

'Don't worry. You couldn't have made yourself any plainer if you'd written a book. You're nothing but a damned tease, Carey. But you aren't going to fly out of here and set every gossipy tongue in the place talking!'

'If you don't want gossip, Brandon, then don't make passes in public places,' Carey spat. She jerked her arm out of his grip and flounced out of the alcove.

Elliot and Gail were still wrangling companionably when Brandon pulled Carey's chair out, his exaggeratedly good manners making the gesture seem an insult. It seemed impossible that neither of their guests recognised the change in the atmosphere. Carey refused to look at Brandon for the rest of the evening. Her head ached fearfully, and it seemed for ever before Gail finally suggested they go home.

Carey opened her eyes the next morning and immediately wished that she hadn't. She felt as though she had a giant-sized hangover. From the bathroom she heard water running. Score another one for Anne, she thought. This was definitely a soak-in-the-tub morning. She pushed back the blankets.

It was the first of December, she thought as she crossed to the window. Twenty-five days till Christmas.

Carey stood for a few minutes looking out over the frosty grass. There had been little snow yet this year, just a few flakes that melted as they touched the ground, but the sky looked like a storm was brewing. And the warm fall was definitely gone; winter was starting out colder than usual. She saw the condensation on the glass rooves of the pool area and the greenhouse, and wondered what the gardener had brought her this morning. Then she remembered—today was poinsettia day. The big Christmas party for the vice-presidents was this weekend; today the decorations would start going up.

Twenty-five days till Christmas, the first she would spend with Brandon. She wondered how many more there would be. Would she still be here next Christmas season, or would he have given up on her by then and set her free, and found another woman who would be more willing to give him his child?

It didn't help, this morning, to know that she loved him, even after the scene last night had made it cruelly plain how he felt about her. At least she had her pride left, and it would not allow her to be taken in again.

How long had she loved him? Had the change taken place at some indefinable moment since their marriage, or did it go even further back? Had the emotions stirring within her been masked by the anger and resentment he had always provoked in her?'

'It's pointless to worry about it,' she told herself, and went to take her bath.

It helped; Carey emerged from the hot water with her headache gone. If the pain in my heart would just go away, too, she thought morosely. She still couldn't believe what had happened last night, and what it had revealed of Brandon. But she should have known—should have expected that if blackmail and threats didn't work he would again try persuasion.

Anne was arranging Carey's hair when the telephone rang. She answered it and turned to Carey. 'It's Miss Forsythe, Mrs Scott.'

Carey sighed. What did Lynne want this time? At least it had better not be money, she told herself.

Lynne was panicky and half-hysterical again today. 'Carey? Can you meet me at the airport at eleven-thirty? I'm flying out on a commuter run to Denver at eleven-forty-five and I have to talk to you. It'll only take a minute.'

'Can't you just tell me about it?'

'Not on the phone, Carey. Just come, please?'

When Lynne said please, it was always serious. 'All right, I'll come. But it had better be important.'

'It is, Carey. It really is.' And Lynne hung up.

A few minutes later, Carey descended the stairs, wearing a lightweight wool dress in cherry-red that she hoped would brighten her spirits, and glanced at her watch. She had half an hour before she had to leave for the airport, so she could supervise the decorations that were going up for Christmas.

She turned the corner into the big drawing room and stopped dead. Two maids on ladders were hanging blue ornaments on an aluminium tree that brushed the ceiling. Another maid was handing up more ornaments.

Carey took a bulb out of the maid's hand. 'Go get Mrs Whitney and bring her to me,' she ordered. 'And then drag the gardener out of the greenhouse and get him in here.'

Mrs Whitney arrived in less than sixty seconds. 'Yes, Mrs Scott?'

Carey didn't look at her. She was still staring at the tree. 'What is that thing?' she demanded.

'It's . . . a Christmas tree.' Mrs Whitney sounded a little doubtful.

'It's a glorified aluminium television antenna, and I refuse to allow it in my house. Get it out of here!'

'But we've used it for several years . . .'

'Good. Then you don't have to feel wasteful about sending it to St. Teresa's orphanage. Or give it to the electronics department at the college—they can make circuits out of it. In fact, I don't care what you do with it as long as you get it out of this house.' She turned and saw the gardener. 'Can you get me a Christmas tree? I mean a real live green one, with needles and everything?'

'Of course, madam.'

'Good. Go get it. And Mrs Whitney? Are there any ornaments in this house? I don't mean four thousand identical blue bulbs, either. I mean ornaments that have some originality, and some sentiment, and some meaning attached to them.'

'Yes, madam.'

'You can start with whichever attic has the things from my apartment. There are a couple of boxes there. And lights, Mrs Whitney. Lots of lights. And tinsel! I'll even put the tinsel on myself. I like to put it on one strand at a time.'

'Yes, madam.' The housekeeper's voice was faint.

'I'll be back in an hour or so, and I'll be in a lot better mood if the windmill there is gone.' Without a backward glance Carey left the room.

The drawing room was quiet. The maids stood in a group, darting looks at Mrs Whitney, who looked as if she had been hit by a truck. Then, suddenly, the housekeeper shook her head and stood up straight. 'You all heard Mrs Scott,' she announced. 'Let's get moving.'

Lynne was not at the airport.

Carey finally checked at the flight desk and was told that her sister's flight had cleared the tower ten minutes before they were to meet.

'It was early, wasn't it?' Carey asked, making a mental note to ask Clarke about it. Being on time was an airline's dream, but flights that left early were no way to please customers. They tended to get upset if the plane left without them.

'No, madam,' the sales clerk said. 'In fact, it was about fifteen minutes late taking off.'

So Lynne had goofed up her times again. Carey told herself not to feel uneasy about it; it wasn't the first time Lynne had done it.

She started for the front door, hoping to pick up a cab. She had told the chauffeur not to wait for her, because she hadn't known how long she would be with Lynne, and Brandon needed the car that afternoon. It was just as well, anyway, Carey told herself. She would much rather take a cab than share the limousine with Brandon. She was just getting a little spoiled about having the car always at her call.

As she was leaving the terminal building, a tall man in a dark blue pilot's uniform, with a topcoat over his arm, pushed open the door of a phone booth and followed her with a leisurely stride. He caught up with her on the sidewalk. 'Carey!' he called. 'What brings you back to the old haunts?'

'Hello, David. I was supposed to meet Lynne, but she messed up on the time, and her plane has gone.'

'That sounds like Lynne.'

'But it sounded important. You wouldn't know what it was she wanted, would you?'

'I haven't any idea. In fact, I haven't seen her since yesterday.' He glanced at his watch. 'Can I take you to lunch, or do you have plans? Maybe we can figure out what it was that Lynne had on her mind.'

'No, I don't have any plans. But you must have other things to do, David.'

'Can't think of a one. Do you have a car here?'

'No, I sent it home. I was going to take a cab.'

'That settles it. We'll have lunch and then I'll take you home.' He took her arm and ushered her towards the parking lot.

It might be a good idea, Carey told herself. She seldom saw David without Lynne around, and this might give her a chance to get to know him better. Maybe he wasn't at all what she thought. 'All right.'

'There's a little place up the river I think you'll like.' He turned the car out of the lot.

'That seems a long way to go.'

'It's worth it.'

He drove fast and they soon left St Louis and followed a winding two-lane highway that ran along the Mississippi River. Carey watched the frozen roadside slip by the car, and shivered.

'Cold?' David asked.

'Oh, a little.' The car heater didn't seem to be working properly. Her leather coat was warm enough when she wore a sweater under it, but she hadn't expected the biting cold and wind that today had brought. Maybe Nancie was right—fur seemed an awfully good idea just now.

'I got caught unprepared this winter,' David said. 'Should have had the heater worked on in this car, but I didn't get around to it.'

'It creeps up on you. What's this place you're taking me to?'

'I'd rather surprise you. Then you won't be disappointed.'

She looked out again at the river, still flowing but only sluggishly. It wouldn't be long until it would freeze upstream, trapping some of the barges that relied on the river highway.

'What routes are you flying these days?' she asked, almost at random.

He seemed to explode. 'Much you care, once you got me kicked off your precious Brandon's plane!'

Carey was stunned by the pent-up anger in his voice. 'What do you mean?'

David's jaw worked convulsively, but then he smiled with a tremendous effort. 'Nothing,' he said. 'I'm on the South American run now. In fact, I leave tonight for Buenos Aires. I won't be back for a while.'

The sudden change was shocking, as if he had been goaded into showing his anger, then promptly put the fence back around his emotions. Carey wondered if he was like this often. Was he violent with Lynne?

Before she could reply, he had pulled the car into a driveway and had shut off the engine.' 'Here we are,' he said genially.

She looked around. All she could see was a small frame house, one of many such summer cabins built along the banks and even down to the river's edge. She turned to face him. 'I don't see . . .'

And then she saw the gun.

CHAPTER ELEVEN

DAVID was pointing the muzzle of the snub-nosed little handgun straight at her face, and he wore an unpleasant smile.

'Now let's go inside quietly, shall we?' he said. 'Not that screaming would do you any good; there is nobody to hear you. But it would be a shame if I had to ruin that lovely face, wouldn't it?'

Carey said, 'What do you think you're doing?'

'Making my fortune. Slide across the seat, now, and get out by my door.'

Carey obeyed. David's gun might be a small one, but she didn't see how he could miss at that range.

She got out of the car and climbed the steps to the reached over her shoulder to push the door open. The inside of the cabin was dark, and there was a musty smell about it.

'Sit down while I light a fire,' David ordered.

Carey didn't see any other option, so she sat down on a straight wooden chair. It at least looked cleaner than the upholstered couch. This must be where David spent his fishing vacations. Fishing for what, she wondered.

He put a match to an already-laid fire, then came to pull up another chair opposite her. 'Now let's have a little brother-sister chat,' he suggested.

'We could have done that on the phone.' That she could speak at all was probably a minor miracle, she decided. Maybe it was true—when faced with an emergency, people could perform beyond their ordinary capabilities.

'Lynne and I have been doing a lot of talking lately, and we decided that it wasn't proper for Brandon to have your sister and brother-in-law on his payroll.'

'I don't imagine Lynne will be turning down the trust

164

fund he's going to offer her,' Carey said tartly.

'That's a little different,' he said.

'And Brandon's stepfather works for him, so I don't think you will convince him that it's improper.'

'All right, smarty, you'll pay for that. The price just went up.'

'Price?'

'We'd have been content for you to turn over the settlement Scott made on you. My information says it's a good size. But I hear it's tied up in trust. I also hear that if anything happens to you, it goes back to him.'

'You're right.' Obviously he knew all the details. Carey searched her memory. She didn't think she had ever mentioned the trust fund to Lynne. She certainly hadn't confided the details about how the plan was set up; she hadn't considered that to be anyone else's business. So how did David know?

'If it isn't too nosey of me, just how did you get all of this information?' she asked.

David grinned. 'It's perfectly easy. You're quite charming, Carey, but with as many people as you have working at your little brick dream-cottage, someone is always unhappy, or jealous, and ready to talk to anyone who wants to listen. Of course when my little friend let her greed get the better of her, and was foolish enough to get caught, it slowed me down.'

'The maid I fired,' Carey mused.

He nodded. 'Just in case you're wondering, she didn't know why I was so interested. She was just happy to have my attention. At any rate, she really messed up my plans. So Lynne and I considered the life assurance idea, but you look plenty healthy to me, and insurance companies usually investigate accidents, especially if they happen soon after the policy is issued.'

Carey didn't answer. She swallowed hard, remembering the way Lynne had brought up the subject of life assurance. It hadn't quite rung true, then, she thought; it wasn't Lynne's style to be thinking about the future. But Carey had been too trusting to be suspicious.

'To tell the truth, we'd almost given up on getting anything from you. But then dear Brandon gave Lynne her marching orders, and we just couldn't sit still for that. So we decided to take the quickest way.' He pulled a small tape recorder and a folded slip of paper from his pocket. 'You just read this into the tape-recorder, and I'll go call Brandon dear, and if he pays up, I'll tell him where you are. If not, well . . .'

'I wouldn't bet on him doing it,' Carey said steadily. 'I'm not exactly in Brandon's good graces today.' She wondered what made David think he could get away with this. Perhaps he had no intention of telling anyone where she was. After all, she could certainly identify her kidnapper.

He seemed to have read her mind. 'I don't think you'd like to see your precious little sister spend the rest of her life in prison,' he reminded gently. 'And if you bring me down, I'll drag her with me. She's in this up to her little chin.'

Carey didn't doubt that he would implicate Lynne, but she wondered if he really thought that her blind love for her sister would keep her silent.

'Let's not delay, now,' he said. 'Put on your saddest voice, Carey.'

Carey read the statement, but David decided she didn't sound scared enough so he made her do it over. The second time her knees were trembling in earnest, and the voice on the tape quavered.

David played the message back and grinned. 'That should wring his hard little heart,' he said. 'Now if you'll just put your hands back here behind the chair . . .'

Carey, dazed, complied. 'I'll take the ring,' he said, pulling the diamond and sapphire engagement ring from her finger. 'You can keep the wedding band. I never was too crazy about those.'

She felt as if she were in a nightmare. This kind of thing didn't happen. But the jerk of her wrists as David tied them together and then to the chair told her that it was all too real, and she started to cry.

'I'd suggest that you not do that, sweetheart,' he said silkily. 'Tears don't move me, and there's going to be nobody here to help you blow your nose.'

He tied her ankles to the chair legs. 'Lynne should have suggested that you wear jeans and a sweater,' he added. 'Not very thoughtful of her, was it? It may get a little cold up here before the rescue party arrives. But I'll build up the fire and you'll be all right.' He put another log on and said, 'Bye, sis. See you around.'

Anne Grover wandered into the big drawing room where the twelve-foot Norwegian pine was beginning to take on the appearance of an old-fashioned Christmas tree.

'Has Mrs Scott come home?' she asked the house-keeper, who was head-first into a box of ornaments.

'I don't believe so. Perhaps she went shopping.'

'But she said . . .' Anne realised belatedly that her counsel had best be kept to herself. Perhaps Mrs Scott had stopped to shop. Or perhaps her sister had been more demanding than usual.

The front doorbell pealed, and Anne hastened to answer it. It certainly wasn't her job, but Whitney was on a ladder stringing lights on Mrs Scott's tree, and there was no point in pulling rank.

The young photographer who had had the run of the house stood on the doorstep. 'I've brought Mrs Scott's pictures,' he said, pushing a box at her. 'I know she was anxious to have her portraits finished by Christmas. Tell her if she can decide by the end of the week I can have them for sure by the holidays.

'Of course,' Anne said, and closed the door behind him. Taking the box to Carey's morning room, she searched for scissors and clipped the string. Mrs Scott would be furious if she ever found out that every package that came into the house was searched before she received it. But then Anne had no intention of telling her that it was part of her maid's job description.

*   *   *

Carey sniffed twice, defiantly, after she heard the car drive away. David had been right about one thing, she decided. She had better keep her head, or when they came to rescue her she would be a raving maniac. How long would it take for the ransom call to be made, for Brandon to come up with a million dollars in cash, and for the rescuers to arrive? She figured it out three times, and the soonest she could be rescued was late evening. The possibility that Brandon might not pay the ransom she didn't consider at all. She didn't dare.

Three o'clock. Lisa, the appointments secretary with the throaty voice, picked up her coffee cup and started towards the outer office and the lounge where the coffee-pot was perking. But as she started to close the door behind her, the telephone on her desk rang.

'I need to talk to Scott,' a male voice said abruptly when she answered.

Another big shot, she muttered. 'I'm sorry, sir, he's in conference. Could you leave your name . . .'

'I'll leave a message,' he interrupted. 'Get your pencil, sweetheart; you might want to take some notes.'

Lisa's pencil was already in her hand, but she was frozen in shock as another voice came on the line. 'Brandon, it's Carey. I've been kidnapped . . .'

Then, with the urging of long training, the pencil point began to move.

She should have fought. She should have kicked and clawed and scratched . . .

And got yourself killed, she told herself. 'No way you could have taken a gun away from a two-hundred-pound pilot who used to play football, Carey,' she said aloud. It was some comfort to hear a voice, even if it was her own. 'At least this way you'll be alive to be rescued.'

In the fireplace a log burned in two and settled with a thud into the bed of embers.

Brandon's chair was tipped back, his feet on the edge of

his desk. Across the desk Clarke and Doug Mason sat. Brandon pulled his glasses off to rub the bridge of his nose and laid them on the blotter.

'It sounds as if you've covered all the angles, Doug. The delivery date is the important thing, of course . . .'

The door burst open and Lisa came in. 'Mr Scott . . .'

'I'm in conference, Lisa.'

'Mrs Scott has been kidnapped. I just got a ransom call.'

Brandon's feet hit the floor. He reached for the telephone and was dialling as he said, 'Are you certain?' .

'I'm positive. It was her voice; it must have been on tape. I took it all down.'

He nodded. 'Whitney? Is Mrs Scott at home?' He tapped a pencil on the blotter. 'I see. I'll call back in a few minutes; make sure Anne Grover is there..I want to talk to her.' He pushed the intercom button. 'Get the security chief up here on the double and tell him to come straight in.' Then he slammed the phone down. 'They were expecting her back at September Hill two hours ago.'

'I should have known it would end up like this,' Doug Mason said bitterly, jumping up to pace the floor. 'I knew there was something wrong with this marriage right from the beginning . . .'

Brandon shot a look at him, but didn't waste time in words. Clarke muttered, 'Doug, remember who you're talking to.' But even he seemed distant, his eyes still on Brandon.

'Tell me what she said, Lisa,' Brandon demanded.

'It was a man first—he wanted to talk to you. Then he said he'd leave a message. There was a click like a tape recorder being turned on, and Mrs Scott said . . .'

'You're certain it was Carey?'

She nodded. 'There's no doubt in my mind.' She glanced down at the pad she held. 'She said "Brandon, it's Carey. I've been kidnapped. Don't call the police. Just get one million dollars in used fifties and twenties. At six o'clock tonight take it to the phone booth at the corner of Seventeenth and Ransom . . .'

'God! We have to get a kidnapper with a sick sense of humour!' Clarke exploded.

' "You'll be called and told what to do next. Be sure you're alone, and drive the Lincoln. The phone booth is being watched; any attempt to install a tap and the deal is off. After the ransom is delivered you'll be told how to find me." ' Lisa put the notebook down. 'It was kind of broken off, as if the recorder was shut off while she was still talking, and then the phone went dead.'

'Get that typed up right away. Security will want to see it.' Brandon strode over to the window and looked out over the city. 'Carey . . .' he said softly. 'Carey . . .'

In all the detective movies she had ever seen the heroine could break free by wriggling out of her bonds. Carey thought there should be enough stretch to allow her to work free.

There wasn't. David apparently knew what he was doing, or perhaps he had just watched the same movies she had. She started to giggle, and stopped, horrified. If she gave in to hysterics she might never stop.

The flames were dying down, and she wondered how long it would be before the cold started to penetrate her coat.

'Who's got a grudge against you now?' It wasn't a flippant question; the security chief, who was sitting at the conference table in Brandon's office, was an ex-FBI agent. 'Better yet, who has a grudge against Mrs Scott?'

'I asked her maid—you know, the policewoman. There's an upstairs maid that Carey fired a couple of weeks ago for pilfering things from her room. That's all. Oh, you might check out a hanger-on she picked up in Washington a month ago. He showed up yesterday, all sweetness and charm.'

'Name?'

'Elliot Lang. He's staying at the Hilton.'

'How about the sister we've been checking up on?'

'No. Lynne's selfish, but she isn't dumb.'

The security man shrugged. 'Then chances are it's somebody getting back at you. Anybody new?'

Brandon ran a hand over the back of his neck. 'No. You've got the list.'

'I think we'd better call in the FBI.'

'She said no cops.' The security man merely looked at him. 'All right. Call.'

'Can you get the million? They'll want to go ahead with the drop.'

Brandon smiled without humour. 'That's the least of my problems right now.'

'Brandon, have you got in touch with Lynne? Anne Grover says Carey went to the airport to meet her. Perhaps she'll know where Carey was going.'

'She's in Denver, Mother. She's flying back on the shuttle tonight anyway. We'll wait till she's back.'

'For God's sake, Brandon, the girl's sister has been kidnapped!'

'I'm aware of that, Mother.' His tone was impatient.

'Don't you think you should tell her? All right, let's not argue. Why don't you send the plane out after her? If you don't want to shock her about Carey, then tell her somebody's ill.'

Brandon snapped his fingers. 'Thanks. I will.' He hung up the phone and turned to the security chief. 'Tell Lynne that Clarke's had a heart attack. He's close enough. And send my jet out to pick her up.'

The man grunted. 'Is the money ready?'

'I can pick it up in fifteen minutes.'

'Brandon, we don't think you should make the drop.'

'You said they would want me to.'

'They want the drop made, but they don't want you to make it. They think—and I do too—that the whole idea may be to get you alone.'

'So they can kill me? There are plenty of chances to do that. Why drag Carey into it?'

'Because they know you'll stop thinking rationally if

she is in danger.'

'Then they're wrong.'

'I'm not so sure.'

Brandon was on his way to the door. He turned. 'I'm making the drop. You may be right—but if you're wrong and our kidnapper recognises a double, we'll never get Carey back. I'd rather risk being killed than to sit safely at home and wait for Carey to die. That would be the worst kind of cowardice, and I am not a coward.'

Mrs Whitney's mouth was thin as she picked up another ornament to hang on the Norwegian pine.

'How can you just keep hanging things on that tree as if nothing is wrong?' one of the maid burst out.

Mrs Whitney didn't miss a motion. 'Because decorating this tree was the last thing Mrs Scott told me to do,' she said simply. 'And it will be ready for her when she comes back.'

Nancie Dennis turned from the long window where she had been looking out into the early twilight. Almost six, she thought. Brandon will be waiting at the phone booth.

She walked across the room and put an arm about the maid's shaking shoulders. 'Let's all pitch in,' she said. 'And let's have every light, every ornament, every strand of tinsel be a prayer for Mrs Scott's safe homecoming.'

Anne Grover, who was sitting by the fireplace with a handkerchief twisted in her hand and the album of Carey's pictures in her lap, laid the album on the hearth, tucked the handkerchief in her pocket, and picked up a handful of tinsel.

Carey was counting strands of tinsel too, as she decorated a tree in her mind. First the lights . . . lots and lots of lights to twinkle on and off. Then ornaments. In her mind she browsed through the boxes that held her Christmas decorations, the elves that sat on her dressing table, the Santa sleigh and reindeer centrepiece, the red velvet stocking with her name on it that she hung each Christmas Eve.

Did Brandon have a Christmas stocking? Of course not, she told herself. Anybody who would own an aluminium Christmas tree wasn't sentimental enough to want a red velvet stocking. She'd have to get him one.

If she was home for Christmas.

It was the first time she had called September Hill "home" and meant it.

'The phone is tapped, Mr Scott. We'll know exactly where you're told to go. The danger comes if he sends you to another phone.'

'I thought he was watching the booth.'

The FBI agent smiled. 'It's tapped at the branch office of the phone company, and there's an agent standing by. Our kidnapper doesn't know as much about this racket as he thinks he does.'

Brandon replayed the conversation in his mind as he waited for the telphone to ring. At his feet was a big attaché case packed to bursting with twenty and fifty dollar bills, the value a kidnapper had put on Carey's life.

He hoped the kidnapper didn't know as much about the racket as that young FBI man did.

The telephone rang.

The fire was dying down. Carey occupied herself for a short time counting the flames that still flickered now and then. She discovered that by wriggling her feet she could push the chair along the floor. But in fifteen minutes she had travelled only a foot closer to the fireplace, and her ankles were aching from the effort. Besides, the method was unsteady at best. She had nearly tipped the chair over once. If she had been closer to the fireplace and had tipped herself into the coals—it was too horrible to think about.

Brandon's eyes grew accustomed to the dark as he drove

the Lincoln out along the winding, almost deserted street. It was a good neighbourhood, similar to the area of the city where September Hill was, but on the far side of town. Was this another example of the puckish sense of humour the kidnapper seemed to display?

He reviewed his instructions. The muffled voice had told him to drive to a particular intersection, to go through the crossing and past five houses, to stop the car, set the attaché case in the gutter, and drive on. He was not to get out of the car, and he was not to dawdle, but to go on to September Hill and wait for the call that would tell him where Carey was. It was one thing the kidnapper and the FBI agreed on.

Brandon had no intention of getting out of the car. He was determined to follow the instructions to the letter. If only the others who had heard them over the telephone tap were as careful! They had promised him they wouldn't interfere, but he had no great faith in the promise. And, after all, they dealt with this sort of thing every day.

He went through the intersection as the yellow light went red, and started counting houses. He saw now why the kidnapper had chosen this part of town; the fifth house was set back from the street beside a ravine, and there was a curve in the street to each side. No one could see this section at all unless they were on the half-block already.

Brandon stopped the car, set the attaché case into the gutter, slammed the door and drove on.

The cop in the black-and-white patrol car watched as the green Lincoln slid through the light.

'They guy must be crazy,' he thought. 'Or drunk. He didn't even see me.' He turned on to the cross street as soon as traffic allowed and speeded up to pursue the Lincoln. The driver hadn't actually run the light, but a warning would not be out of place.

A hundred feet ahead his lights picked out a suitcase sitting at the edge of the street. He'd better get it out of the way; it shouldn't be hard to catch the Lincoln yet.

He pulled off to the side and had just picked up the case when a voice behind him said, 'I'll take that off your hands, Officer.'

Instinct came to his aid. He dived, rolled, and came up with his gun. Pain stabbed through him as a bullet cut through his chest, and he pulled the trigger of his service revolver.

Carey had decorated her Christmas tree twice and was involved in making out her gift list. The fire was gone, even the glowing embers crumbling into grey ash, and she was getting stiff and hungry. The early winter dark had fallen and the room was almost black.

'In a manner of speaking,' Carey told herself aloud, 'I couldn't see my hand in front of my face even if I could put my hand in front of my face.'

The cold was creeping into her body insidiously now. Her hands and feet were numb. 'Next time you go out to lunch in December, Carey,' she scolded, 'wear something a little warmer than high-heeled sandals. You should have listened to Emily Post.'

She was shivering. She tried to tell herself that hypothermia—the loss of body heat—wasn't serious until the body stopped shivering, but it didn't make her feel any warmer.

The unmarked FBI car skidded to a stop behind the black-and-white patrol car, and all four doors flew open. The first agent to reach the cop turned to call, 'Get an ambulance!'

The second went on to the other man, sprawled on the verge of the road, hand still clutching the attaché case. The agent reached for the fallen man's wrist and swore. 'He's dead. Damn, we lost it all!'

CHAPTER TWELVE

HER arms were cramped and aching. Carey tried to relax the muscles, but she was too tense. How dumb can one woman be? she thought, and righteous indignation at herself made her blood flow faster. 'If you'd been thinking all along, you'd have known David was a rotter,' she scolded herself. Lynne had always been spoiled and demanding, but she had never been so bad before she took up with him.

No, Carey said in self-defence, but there was never the opportunity before either. Carey had always held a good job, but it hadn't held out the possibility of million-dollar payoffs.

Anybody should have put two and two together, though. Why hadn't she remembered? Lynne had told her David was on the plane when Millicent Ayres' necklace had been stolen. Then David had told her himself that he was flying against the rules. No wonder he had thought Carey was responsible for the loss of his position. And no wonder the blame had fallen on Lynne for stealing the necklace—it must have been David.

Unless it had been Lynne . . . and Carey found herself wondering just how much Lynne knew.

'Nothing yet.' Nancie guided Brandon to the chair beside the drawing room fireplace. 'Did it go off all right?'

'Fine. There should be a call any minute.'

Instead, Whitney came to the door. 'Mr Scott? Miss Britton and Mr Lang are here . . .'

Nancie saw Brandon's face start to crumble and moved quickly to the door. She took Gail and Elliot by the arms and guided them back into the hall.

'Here's your hat, what's your hurry?' Elliot asked.

'We were invited . . .'

But Gail saw the tension in Nancie's face. 'Shut up, Elliot. What's going on?' she demanded.

'Carey's been kidnapped. Brandon just came back from delivering the ransom, and we're waiting for the call to tell us where she is.'

'Oh, God.' Elliot hit himself in the head. 'Poor Princess.'

'And poor Brandon,' Gail added.

'Come into the drawing room. I don't think Brandon could stand hearing it again. We're decorating the Christmas tree.' Nancie tried to smile at the amazed looks she got. 'Carey demanded an old-fashioned tree this morning, just before she left. We're going to have her home by the time it's finished.'

'Then let's go help, Elliot.' Gail took him by the arm.

If I get out of this, Carey told herself sombrely, I'm not wasting any more time on pride. So what if Brandon doesn't love me? I love him, and perhaps if I have his child he'll learn to care about me. Stranger things have happened. A man has a special relationship with the woman who carries his child, and even if it isn't love, it will have to do, she thought. Surely he'd let me stay with him then; surely he wouldn't separate me from my baby.

For a moment she was lost in pleasant thought. 'Why all the worry about what to give a millionaire for Christmas?' she quipped. 'Just give him what he wants most!'

If that's what he still wants, she added. After last night's argument he might have changed his mind. Well, she'd worry about that after she got out of this.

If I get out of this, she repeated, and tears began to slide down her cheeks. 'Oh, Brandon, I love you,' she sobbed. 'Will you ever know?'

Elliot and Gail were hanging tinsel as if attempting to make up for lost time. Nancie had turned to the window, the curtains still open to the night.

Brandon sat in front of the fireplace, listlessly flipping through the album Anne had left there. On every page Carey smiled out at him. Was this to be his only remembrance of her? In the park, in the pool, on the grand staircase; in formal gown, in slacks and ski sweater. The pictures went on and on. They tormented him but he could not lay the book down. And still the phone was silent.

The security chief and the young FBI agent were in the room before he was aware. The security man laid a hand on Brandon's shoulder. 'I have some bad news,' he said.

'She's dead?'

'No . . . we don't know. But the kidnapper is dead. A uniformed cop got between him and the ransom, and he panicked and shot the cop. On his way down, the cop fired back. He was a better shot.'

'You're sure it was the kidnapper?'

'Yes. This was in his pocket.' The man handed Brandon the marquise diamond Carey had worn.

Brandon turned it in the firelight, then idly slid it on to his little finger. 'It's hers, all right. And now the only one who knew where she is is dead.'

'Maybe not, Brandon. Your mother's instincts may have been right.'

'What do you mean?'

'Lynne may know. And that plane will land in less than half an hour. The man we got was David Stratton.'

Carey hated the dark. It was harder to stay alert when it was dark, because there was nothing to look at. Her arms weren't hurting any more. Nothing was hurting. And she knew, foggily, that she had to stay awake. The little she had read about hypothermia had been definite on that.

'You have to stay awake, Carey,' she told herself in a mumble. 'They'll come . . .'

Unless she was waiting in vain. Unless there had been no ransom demand made, or David had been scared off, or Brandon had refused to pay . . .

'Stop that!' she told herself, and had the bitter comfort of knowing she was wide awake for a few minutes at least.

The big jet taxied to the landing area that had been roped off for it, and the engines were still running when Brandon, with Gail and the FBI men at his heels, ran up the steps.

Lynne was waiting to debark. 'I can't imagine why Clarke is calling for me,' she complained as Brandon came on board. 'I was never his favourite; Carey is.'

'Clarke's fine. It's Carey you were called back for. She's been kidnapped, and your beloved David did it.'

'No!'

'Yes. David's dead, Lynne. A cop got between him and the ransom money. David's dead, and the cop isn't much better off. But Carey's still gone.'

'Why do you think I have anything to do with it?' Lynne queried tremulously.

Brandon ignored her. 'We don't know where she is. She may be dying out there, Lynne. She may be out-side—and the wind chill is fourteen below zero. Do you know how long a person can last in that? You're the only one who may have a clue to where she is!'

'I had nothing to do with it. David told me he wanted to talk to her, not anything else! I don't know anything about it.'

'But what little you do know might save Carey's life, Lynne.' Gail took the girl's arm and led her to a chair. 'Come on, honey, think. Where might he have taken her?'

Lynne shrugged. 'It would take for ever.'

'Then let's start. Time is what Carey may not have much of.'

'How do you know it was David?' Lynne demanded.

'Because he shot the cop to get the ransom money, and because this was in his pocket.' Brandon flourished the marquise diamond in Lynne's face. 'Carey was wearing it this morning.'

Lynne was silent.

The security man sat down beside her. 'Lynne, David was scheduled out on a flight to Buenos Aires tonight—he wasn't coming back. And I don't think he'd asked you to join him—had he?'

'Carey has always been there when you needed her, Lynne.' Gail's voice was implacable. 'Now she needs you. Are you going to help her?'

Lynne crumbled. 'His apartment . . .'

'It's been checked. Along with all of Universal's hangars and anything else we can figure out that he had access to.'

Lynne put her head into her hands. 'There's a little cabin up on the river road where he took his vacation . . .'

Carey's head drooped, despite herself. It was too hard to stay awake. What was there to stay awake for, anyway? The ransom should have been paid hours ago. If she was going to be rescued they would have come long ago. Why not just go to sleep? If she died then, in the cold, at least it would be without torment.

A door slammed, and that was the first Carey realised that the hum she had been hearing—the hum of a well-tuned Lincoln—hadn't been her imagination. Then hasty footsteps sounded on the porch, and a flashlight flickered around the room.

'Carey!' Brandon's voice was ragged.

'I'll answer to anything right now,' she murmured.

'Are you all right, Mrs Scott?'

'I'm cold. Just cold.'

'No injuries?'

'No.'

Gentle hands were untying the nylon stockings that held her to the chair, and then massaged her hands and feet. She cried out at the pain. 'It's all prickly!'

'That's good, Carey. The circulation is coming back.'

She was having trouble sorting out the voices, but she knew it was Gail who brought a blanket, the warmest thing she had ever felt. And she knew it was Brandon who carried her out to the Lincoln.

'Brandon?' she said muzzily.

'Yes, my dear?'

If she was struck dead right now, she thought, she would be content just to have heard his voice again.

'Forgive me.'

'For what, Carey?'

'For not trusting you to come. I thought you'd said you wouldn't pay the ransom . . .'

His arms tightened. 'My God, Carey, will you forgive me for taking so long?'

She smiled mistily and went to sleep, her head on his shoulder.

Carey woke to an argument between an FBI agent in the front seat and Brandon in the back.

'I'm taking her home,' Brandon insisted. 'We'll get a doctor to meet us there. I will not put her through an emergency room.'

'She needs medical care, Mr Scott.'

'The girl has had a hell of a day. I'm taking her home, and the hospital can come to her.'

'I think Brandon's right,' Gail said gently. 'Carey, are you awake? Do you think you should stop at a hospital, or do you want to go on home?'

'Home.' The voice was weak, but it was definite.

'See?' Brandon couldn't resist a last jibe.

Nancie Dennis saw the lights of the Lincoln sweep through the front gates. 'They're here,' she announced, unnecessarily, for the others had seen too. They clustered at the window; staff members whose shifts had ended six hours before but who had stayed on, friends who had gathered as the news spread, family represented by Nancie and Clarke and Lynne.

Then, unable to wait, they started for the entrance hall where Whitney was opening the door to admit Brandon, carrying a blanket-wrapped Carey. 'Welcome home, madam,' the butler said, his calm restored after a day that had seen him as upset as the rest.

'Brandon?' Nancie started forward. 'Is she . . .'

'Hi, Nancie. Everybody,' Carey said weakly. 'How nice of you to drop in.'

Nancie turned, sobbing, into Clarke's arms.

'Is Lynne all right?'

Lynne came slowly through the group, her eyes swollen and red, her fists clenched on a handkerchief that had ripped under her nails. 'Carey, will you ever be able to forgive me?' she whispered.

Carey lifted a hand and stroked her sister's cheek. 'We'll talk tomorrow, Lynne,' she promised. 'Mrs Whitney?'

'Yes madam?'

'Is that awful tree out of my house?'

Nancie gathered her composure and turned to Whitney. 'Light the tree,' she said. 'Our Carey has come home.'

CHAPTER THIRTEEN

CAREY sipped her hot chocolate and set the mug back on the bedside table. 'Is there anybody else waiting out there to see me?'

'No one, Mrs Scott.' Anne was shaking out the bed-jacket that she had insisted Carey put on before the FBI agent had come in to talk to her.

Carey had thought the whole thing ridiculous and had offered to go out to the sitting room to talk to the man, but Anne had been firm. 'The doctor said you were to stay in bed all day today,' she had said. 'And you're staying.' Anne hadn't forgiven herself yet for her part in Carey's kidnapping and she was determined not to slip up again.

'I know you think it's been a circus already this morning.' Not only had the agent been in, but Lynne had sobbed out her story on her sister's shoulder and been forgiven.

Carey was certain she had done the right thing in forgiving Lynne. She had learned a hard lesson by losing David, her faith in him, and almost losing her sister in one blow. Carey believed Lynne's declaration of innocence, but what was even more important, the FBI believed her too.

But Carey was certain of one thing: Lynne would never manoeuvre her again. Gail had been right all along; it was no favour to Lynne to be too lenient with her. Lynne was still a child, a child Carey had never made grow up.

Nancie had also been in briefly, and Gail, and there had been more phone calls than she could count.

But there had not been so much as a word from Brandon. Carey thoughtfully sipped the hot chocolate again. Maybe he had gone on to the office while she slept, and he would stop by at lunchtime. Maybe he was still asleep. Maybe he didn't care if he saw her.

Maybe he was with Michelle, she thought, or whichever woman had replaced her. Carey sighed. She would have to be careful about that; if she let him see the stab of jealousy she was bound to feel a dozen times a day, he would never allow her to stay at September Hill. Jealousy was the first thing that bored him, he had said.

Had she imagined the tender way he had held her last night, the way he would not put her down even in the drawing room when he had taken her in to admire the tree? Had he been reluctant to let go of her, or did it just seem that way because she wanted it?'

She stirred restlessly in the big bed. 'Can't I get up, Anne?'

'No, Mrs Scott. Would you like a fresh negligee and your hair brushed?'

'If that's the best you can offer.' Then, penitently, 'I'm sorry, Anne. I'd have given my right arm yesterday to have you brush my hair, and today I'm complaining again.'

There was a knock at the door, and Carey sat up straighter, her heart thumping. Surely this would be Brandon!

But after a whispered conference outside the door, Anne returned with a low bowl of daisies and baby's breath to set beside Carey's bed. 'From the greenhouse,' she explained unnecessarily.

Carey dutifully admired the flowers, but her heart wasn't in it. 'Just leave my hair down for now, Anne. And would you go down to the kitchen and get me some more hot chocolate?'

'I'll call and have some brought up.'

'Anne, please. I'm not a baby, and I won't disappear as soon as your back is turned.'

The moment Anne was gone Carey pushed the blankets back and got out of bed. The sun was streaming down brightly over the lawn. How she longed to go and take a swim, but she supposed there was a reason for the order to stay in bed. Tomorrow, for sure, she decided.

A tap sounded at the door and she turned to call 'Come in,' then grimaced at herself. That's all she needed, to be caught breaking the rules, and Anne wouldn't stir from her side again.

But it was Brandon. 'I've been waiting for ever for the dragon to leave,' he said.

'She went to get me some hot chocolate. You could have told her to go away.'

'As touchy as she is today, I wouldn't dare. May I come in?'

'Of course.' She nervously brushed her hair back over her shoulder. He looked so tall, standing there in a Scandinavian ski sweater over an open-necked shirt and dark trousers. His eyes swept over her low-cut negligee, and Carey stood up proudly under his gaze. She knew her colour had returned this morning and that she looked good in the emerald green satin. She wondered what Brandon thought of it.

'I forgot to give this back to you last night in all the confusion.' He pulled the marquise diamond off his finger.

'Oh—thank you!' Carey slipped it on to her hand next to the wide wedding band. 'I was feeling lonely without it.'

'Were you?'

Why did he sound so cold? 'Sit down, Brandon, please.' She sat down herself in one of the velvet chairs by the window. He followed suit—reluctantly, she thought. 'The FBI man told me where they found it.'

'Did they tell you that David's dead?'

'Yes. How is the policeman he shot?'

'He's holding his own after surgery last night. I talked to his wife this morning.'

'I'd like to see him.'

'I'll take you tomorrow, if you like.' He stared out of the window. 'They have two small children.'

'I think they should have an extra-nice Christmas.'

'I thought you'd feel that way.'

Carey was silent a moment. 'I wish I was sorry about David. I think Lynne will eventually feel the same way, though she's taking it hard now.' She hesitated. 'I've learned my lesson, by the way.'

'What's that?'

'That sometimes being too generous a giver isn't good for the one who receives. Lynne wanted me to give you a message. She said she'd learned a lesson too, and she isn't interested any more in an allowance, or a trust fund, or whatever it was you had in mind.'

'This might be the making of that young woman.' He was silent for a moment. 'Carey, this isn't going to be easy for me to say. What you said the other evening about me keeping you a prisoner—it really hit me. And then yesterday, knowing that your life was hanging in the balance because you'd married me . . . I made up my mind, finally.'

'You're frightening me.'

He smiled sadly. 'You needn't be frightened of me ever again. You were right all along. Marriage based on nothing more than physical desire is a bad idea—so we're going to end this farce before it hurts us any more.'

Carey's world spun.

'I did a cruel thing when I married you without love. I didn't know until yesterday that Doug Mason loves you. To be honest, if I had, I wouldn't have let it stand in my way. But I've grown up some myself, Carey, and now I know that what I want isn't what's most important. I want you to be happy—that's what is most important to me now.'

Carey opened her mouth to protest, but no words would come.

'You're expecting there will be a price tag, because there always has been.' Brandon's mouth twisted. 'There isn't, Carey. You'll be well provided for—I owe it to you.'

'You don't owe me anything!'

'Then take it to let me salve my conscience. The lawyers will arrange all that.'

As they always do, Carey thought. She tried again. 'Do you want a divorce, Brandon?'

He smiled, a sad, tired smile. 'What I want isn't important just now.'

'It is to me! What about Michelle? and Tony?'

'Michelle?' he questioned, as if he didn't recognise the name. 'Do you mean, am I telling you this long sad story to save my face so that I can marry someone else? No, Carey. Believe it or not—and I know it's hard to believe—there is no other woman. I was trying to make you jealous. Stupid, wasn't it?'

She couldn't speak. It was so much more than she had dreamed of.

Brandon stood up suddenly and went to the window, as if the room was stifling him. 'What really convinced me was when you said your children would be born of love. I had thought perhaps if we had a child I could teach you to love me. I was foolish—love can't be forced.'

'You don't . . . want a child?'

'Of course I do. Our child, Carey. Your child, because you're the woman I love. Ironic, isn't it? I married you to punish you for turning me down—and I'm the one who fell in love.'

She swallowed hard. 'I gave you my word of honour, Brandon. I won't walk out on that.'

He turned swiftly from the window. 'I cheated you, damn it! And I'm freeing you. You don't know what it costs me to say that!'

Her eyes fell before the fire in his. Was it going to take a stick of dynamite to get through to him? Well, she would light a stick and hand it to him.

'All right, Brandon, if that's what you want.'

'It isn't what I want. What I want is to keep you here and pamper and pet you and make love to you and protect you. But I won't keep you in a cage any more.'

Carey's fingers pleated the satin skirt of her gown. 'Are you in a hurry to have this over?'

'The sooner it's finished the less painful it will be.'

'Because I'd like to have a chance to recover from this shock before I start into another upheaval in my life.'

'How long do you need?' His tone was grudging.

'Fifty years should do it.'

There was a long silence.

'And that whole list of things, Brandon? Pampering and petting and making love and so on? If that is keeping me in a cage, then I want to be caged.' She looked up to meet the fire in his eyes, and finished steadily, 'I did a lot of thinking, too. I was less generous than you, because I decided I wanted you whether or not you loved me.'

And then she could say nothing at all, for he was across the room to her, his arms around her, kissing her in a ferocious, almost violent way that threatened to suffocate her, his hands tangled in the long strands of her hair as he held her crushed against him.

She struggled for breath and he loosened his grip instantly, feathering gentle kisses across her cheek and temple as he said, 'You'll stay with me?'

When she could breathe, she murmured, 'Only because you're so odiously wealthy.'

'You'll pay for that,' he threatened, and moulded her body against his.

'I hope so,' Carey said demurely, and let her hands slide across his shoulders to clasp at the back of his neck and pull his head down.

He let his fingers slide through the long chestnut hair. 'I'm so glad you didn't cut your hair,' he murmured.

'How did you know I even considered it? The only person I told was Anne. Is she a spy?' But she forgot the question as he kissed her again.

Long minutes later, Brandon said unsteadily, 'Did the dragon ever come back with your hot chocolate?'

Carey laughed. 'If she did, she must have got the message. Oh, Brandon, I never thought I'd hear you use the word love.'

'You can expect to hear a lot about it in the future.' Suddenly he picked her up.

'What are you doing?'

'Putting you back to bed. You've been up far too long now.'

Carey giggled, but she soon discovered that he meant it. He tucked her in and leaned over to kiss her gently. 'I'll send Anne in with your hot chocolate. If I stay any longer, you won't get any rest—I'll guarantee it. Go to sleep.'

'The doctor just said I had to stay in bed, not that I had to sleep.' She reached up to toy with the top button on his shirt. 'I'm not in the least sleepy, really, Brandon.'

'No?'

'But he did say I was not to be left alone. And Anne has a trillion things to do today.'

'Which you are busy inventing right now. Is this the invitation I've been waiting for?'

'You'd better believe it.'

'In that case . . .' He reached for the telephone beside her bed. 'Whitney?'

Carey heard the butler answer, 'Yes, sir?'

'Please inform the staff that Mrs Scott is not to be disturbed for any reason. And I do mean any reason, Whitney. Particularly hot chocolate.'

'Yes, sir.'

Brandon gently replaced the receiver. 'Now, where were we?' he asked, turning back to his wife.